RESILIENCE IN THE SHADOWS

BY Nazreen Zainab

RESILIENCE IN THE SHADOWS

First edition. September 12, 2024.

Copyright © 2024 Nazreen zainab.

ISBN: 979-8227408839

Written by Nazreen zainab.

Table of Contents

Introduction

"Resilience in the Shadows" is an Islamic romance and thriller novel focused on redemption, personal growth, and finding peace after adversity. It intertwines romance, faith, and humour in a relatable way, guiding readers through a journey of struggle, healing, and love within the boundaries of Islamic teachings.

Main Characters

AALIYAH : A RESILIENT and intelligent woman, from a wealthy family, who has been crushed by her first marriage but emerges stronger. A devout Muslim, she is an Alima (Alima means a Islamic teacher)who values her faith above everything.

Hassan Rafiq: A manipulative, controlling, and abusive first husband who hides behind a religious facade but is the source of Aaliyah's pain.

Zayd Malik: A caring and compassionate man who enters Aaliyah's life after her divorce. He represents the love and peace that Aaliyah has been searching for, bringing out her laughter and faith.

Salma : Aaliyah's cruel and tormenting mother-in-law during her first marriage.

Adnan and Ameen: Aaliyah's two sons, aged 5 and 6, who are her joy and the reason she fights through the darkest moments of her life.

Her Family: Protective and loving, Aaliyah's siblings and parents, who arrange her first marriage but later realize the gravity of their mistake. They become her pillars of support.

Chapter 1

The First Marriage

Scene 1: The Eve of the Wedding

The sun had set on the eve of Aaliyah Hassan's wedding, and the air inside the sprawling estate of the Hassan family was thick with the scent of jasmine and the hum of last-minute preparations. Aaliyah sat in her bedroom, staring out the large window that overlooked the gardens, where strings of fairy lights danced among the trees. Despite the beauty surrounding her, an unsettling feeling of doubt gnawed at the edges of her heart.

Aaliyah was only twenty years old, with her whole life ahead of her. She had been raised in comfort and privilege, attending the finest schools until she chose to immerse herself in religious studies at a renowned madrasa. Her decision to become an Alima was met with pride from her parents, who valued education and faith equally. Now, as she prepared to enter a new chapter of her life, her thoughts were a whirlwind of anxiety and hope.

Her siblings, Safiya and Mohammed , burst into the room, breaking her reverie. Safiya, always the practical one, immediately began fussing over Aaliyah's bridal jewellery, while Malik teased her about the upcoming ceremony. Their laughter filled the room, but Aaliyah's smile felt forced. She loved her family dearly and trusted their decision to arrange her marriage to Hassan Rafiq, a man they described as devout and responsible. But in the quiet corners of her mind, doubt lingered.

After her siblings left, Aaliyah found herself alone once more. She turned to her reflection in the mirror, her long black hair cascading over her shoulders. She was beautiful, as many had told her, but tonight, the beauty felt like a mask hiding her uncertainty. She clasped her hands together, lowering her head in silent prayer.

"O Allah," she whispered, "grant me peace and ease my heart. Guide me through this new chapter in my life."

With that, she rose from her seat, ready to face whatever lay ahead.

SCENE 2: THE GRAND Wedding Ceremony

The next day was a blur of colours, sounds, and emotions as Aaliyah's wedding unfolded in grand fashion. The Hassan family estate was transformed into a palace of celebration, with every corner adorned in rich fabrics and vibrant flowers. Guests arrived in droves, each more elegantly dressed than the last, as they gathered to witness the union of two prominent families.

Aaliyah, dressed in an intricate red and gold bridal gown, sat quietly in the center of the bridal room. The ceremony was about to begin, and her heart raced with a mixture of nerves and anticipation. Her mother entered, her eyes misty with tears of joy, and knelt beside her daughter.

"You look beautiful, Aaliyah," her mother said, gently adjusting the hem of her dress. "Today marks the beginning of a new life for you. Trust in Allah, and He will guide you."

Aaliyah nodded, her voice caught in her throat. Soon, it was time for the nikah, the formal marriage contract. She was led into the main hall, where Hassan awaited her. He stood tall and confident, dressed in traditional attire that spoke of modesty and piety. As Aaliyah approached, their eyes met briefly. Hassan smiled a smile that was warm yet unreadable.

The ceremony proceeded with the recitation of verses from the Quran. Aaliyah's heart thudded in her chest as she repeated her vows, her voice steady despite her inner turmoil. Hassan's voice, too, was strong and assured as he committed to their marriage in front of family, friends, and, most importantly, Allah.

After the vows were exchanged, the room erupted in congratulatory cheers. Aaliyah's parents embraced her, their faces glowing with pride. Her siblings surrounded her, offering their heartfelt blessings. But as Aaliyah looked around, she noticed the subtle distance in the expressions of Hassan's family, particularly his mother, Salma, who offered a cool smile that didn't quite reach her eyes.

"Insha'Allah, you will find peace and happiness in your new home," her mother whispered, hugging her tightly.

Aaliyah clung to her mother for a moment longer, drawing strength from her warmth, before stepping into the unknown with her new husband.

SCENE 3: ENTERING THE New Household

Aaliyah's arrival at Hassan's home was a moment she had both anticipated and dreaded. The house, while smaller than her family's estate, was elegant and well-maintained, reflecting the quiet respectability of Hassan's family. Yet, from the moment she crossed the threshold, Aaliyah felt a sense of unease.

Hassan led her through the house, pointing out various rooms and explaining the routines of the household. Aaliyah nodded along, trying to absorb everything. But it was when she met Salma again that the unease took root.

Salma greeted Aaliyah with a smile that was polite but distant. The older woman was impeccably dressed, her posture rigid with the air of someone used to being in control. She spoke in soft, measured tones, but her words were laced with criticism. She pointed out that Aaliyah's dress was a little too extravagant, that her jewellery was too flashy for everyday wear, and that she hoped Aaliyah knew her way around a kitchen, because in this house, everyone was expected to contribute.

"You may have been spoiled in your father's house," Salma said, her voice carrying a hint of disdain, "but here, we value simplicity and hard work."

Aaliyah felt her cheeks flush with embarrassment. She had always been proud of her upbringing, but here, in this new home, it felt like a liability. She forced a smile, determined to make a good impression despite the chilly reception.

Hassan, meanwhile, seemed oblivious to his mother's tone. He continued to show Aaliyah around, eventually leading her to their bedroom. The room was plain, with a simple bed, a wooden dresser, and a small prayer mat in the corner. It was a stark contrast to the luxurious room she had left behind, but Aaliyah told herself that it didn't matter. This was her new life, and she would embrace it with all her heart.

That night, as they prepared for bed, Hassan sat beside Aaliyah and took her hand in his.

"I know this is a big change for you," he said, his voice gentle. "But you will get used to the way we do things here. My mother can be a bit strict, but she means well. Just remember, as my wife, you must respect her and follow the rules of the house."

Aaliyah nodded, though a part of her bristled at the implication. She had always been taught that a wife should be obedient, but this felt different. There was an underlying expectation of submission that made her uncomfortable.

"Of course," she replied softly. "I will do my best to make this my home."

Hassan smiled, satisfied with her response, and they settled into bed. But as Aaliyah lay there, staring up at the ceiling, she couldn't shake the feeling that she was no longer in control of her own life.

SCENE 4: THE HONEYMOON Period

The first few weeks of Aaliyah's marriage were a time of adjustment. She threw herself into her new role with determination, waking early each morning to help Salma with the household chores. She cooked, cleaned, and did everything she could to prove herself as a capable and dutiful wife.

However, it soon became clear that nothing she did was good enough. Salma's criticisms were constant and unrelenting. If Aaliyah made a dish, Salma would find fault with the seasoning. If she cleaned a room, Salma would point out a missed spot. Aaliyah began to dread every interaction with her mother-in-law, her confidence eroding with each passing day.

Hassan, meanwhile, seemed increasingly distant. He spent long hours at work and, when he was home, he often buried himself in religious texts, leaving little time for conversation. When they did speak, it was usually about the house or their duties as Muslims. Hassan encouraged Aaliyah to spend more time studying religious texts and less time worrying about trivial matters like visiting her family or keeping in touch with friends.

"Your role now is to support me and our future family," he would say. "The outside world is a distraction from your true purpose."

Aaliyah tried to find solace in her faith, praying for patience and understanding. She reminded herself that marriage was about compromise and sacrifice. Yet, the more she tried to adapt, the more isolated she felt.

One evening, after a particularly harsh scolding from Salma over a burned dish, Aaliyah retreated to her room in tears. She hadn't expected marriage to be easy, but she had never imagined it would be this lonely. She missed her family, her friends, and the freedom she once had. But most of all, she missed the sense of self she had lost in this new life.

SCENE 5: FIRST SIGNS of Trouble

The first real argument between Aaliyah and Hassan occurred about three months into their marriage. It started innocently enough, with Aaliyah asking if she could visit her family for a few days. She hadn't seen them since the wedding, and she missed them dearly.

To her surprise, Hassan reacted with anger. He accused her of being selfish and ungrateful, saying that her place was with him and that visiting her family was a luxury she could no longer afford.

"You need to focus on your duties here," Hassan snapped. "Your family

will only distract you from what's important."

Aaliyah was taken aback by his harsh tone. She had always been taught that family was a blessing and that maintaining close ties was part of being a good Muslim. But Hassan's reaction made her question everything she had believed.

"I'm sorry," she said quietly. "I didn't mean to upset you. I just miss them."

Hassan's expression softened slightly, but his words remained firm.

"You need to understand that your life has changed. You are no longer your father's daughter you are my wife. And that comes with responsibilities."

Aaliyah nodded, her heart heavy with disappointment. She had hoped that marriage would bring her closer to her husband, but instead, it seemed to be pushing her further away from the people she loved.

SCENE 6: THE CRACKS Deepen

As the months passed, the cracks in Aaliyah's marriage deepened. Hassan's controlling behaviour became more pronounced, and Salma's torment grew more intense. Aaliyah felt trapped in a life that was suffocating her, with no way to escape.

Her once vibrant personality began to fade, replaced by a quiet resignation. She no longer argued with Hassan or tried to reason with Salma. Instead, she retreated into herself, praying for strength and hoping that things would somehow get better.

But deep down, Aaliyah knew that something had to change. She couldn't continue living like this isolated, controlled, and constantly belittled. She had always believed that marriage was sacred, but now she wondered if staying in this marriage was truly what Allah wanted for her.

One night, as she lay in bed, staring at the ceiling once again, Aaliyah made a decision. She didn't know what the future held, but she knew that she couldn't let this marriage destroy her. She would find a way to reclaim her life, even if it meant walking away from everything she had known.

"O Allah," she whispered into the darkness, "grant me the strength to find my way through this storm."

And with that, Aaliyah closed her eyes, her heart heavy but resolute.

CHAPTER 1 ENDS WITH Aaliyah beginning to recognize the toxicity of her marriage and the inner strength she will need to eventually escape it. The seeds of her resilience are planted, even though she has yet to fully embrace them.

Chapter 2

Beneath the Surface

Scene 1: The Quiet Observations

In the early months of her marriage, Aaliyah continued to struggle with the growing tension in the household. Hassan's presence was sporadic—he often spent long hours at work, and when he was home, he was distant, more interested in his religious books than in her. He showed little curiosity or concern about the interactions between Aaliyah and his mother, Salma. His indifference cut deeply, making Aaliyah feel invisible, but she never dared to voice her concerns. After all, she had been taught that patience and silence were virtues in a wife.

But even as Aaliyah kept silent, she couldn't ignore the cruelty that crept into her life through her mother-in-law's daily actions. Salma's disdain for Aaliyah was subtle at first—small, offhand remarks about her upbringing, veiled criticisms of her family's wealth, and the constant pressure to perform domestic duties to Salma's impossible standards.

"In this house," Salma would say, her voice cold and condescending, "we don't have servants running around to do everything for us. You'll need to learn how to keep things clean on your own."

Salma never raised her voice, but the icy undertone in her words spoke volumes. Aaliyah tried to tell herself that Salma was simply strict, that perhaps her mother-in-law had grown used to a particular way of life. But the cruelty became clearer with each passing day.

SCENE 2: THE DISAPPEARING Meals

It began with the meals. Aaliyah had been taught to cook from a young age, and while her skills weren't as honed as those of someone who had been cooking every day, she was competent enough to prepare a decent meal. But in Salma's eyes, nothing was ever good enough.

When Aaliyah cooked, Salma would quietly watch from the kitchen doorway, never offering help or guidance. She would wait until Aaliyah had finished cooking, and then, just as Aaliyah set the table for dinner, Salma would throw the entire meal away.

"This food is barely edible," Salma would say as she scraped the food into the trash. "I'm doing you a favour. Next time, try harder."

Hassan never questioned why dinner was always delayed. By the time he arrived home from work, Salma had already prepared a new meal, and no one mentioned the earlier incident. Aaliyah would sit at the dinner table in silence, her stomach growling, as Salma made passive-aggressive comments about the importance of a wife knowing her way around the kitchen.

"You're lucky Hassan doesn't complain," Salma would say with a tight smile. "My other sons would never tolerate such incompetence."

Aaliyah wanted to scream, to tell Hassan what was happening, but she feared his reaction. She had seen how little attention he paid to the household. If he didn't care to ask why his mother was cooking meals instead of Aaliyah, what hope did she have that he would care about her suffering?

SCENE 3: ISOLATION and Control

Salma's control extended far beyond the kitchen. Slowly, she began to restrict Aaliyah's movements. Whenever Aaliyah expressed a desire to visit her family, Salma would find a way to intervene.

"Your family can wait," Salma would say with a wave of her hand. "There is too much to do here. Besides, it's not proper for a wife to be running back to her parents' house every time she feels homesick. You belong here now."

Aaliyah felt trapped, cut off from the people who loved her most. She longed to see her mother, to hear her siblings' laughter, but every time she asked, Salma would shut her down. Hassan, when asked, would simply echo his mother's sentiments.

"My mother is right," Hassan would say dismissively. "You're not a child anymore. Your family isn't going anywhere. You have responsibilities here now."

And so, Aaliyah's world shrank. She rarely left the house except for the occasional trip to the market, always accompanied by Salma. Salma ensured that Aaliyah had no privacy, no moments of freedom. She hovered over Aaliyah constantly, monitoring her every move, criticizing every mistake, and ensuring that Aaliyah never felt truly comfortable or at home.

SCENE 4: SABOTAGE AND Manipulation

The cruelty didn't stop with isolation. Salma began to sabotage Aaliyah's efforts around the house in subtle ways. If Aaliyah cleaned a room, Salma would come in afterward and deliberately mess things up—moving furniture, spilling water, and even tearing through Aaliyah's carefully folded laundry.

"This is unacceptable, "Salma would say, pointing to the mess. "You can't even clean properly. What kind of wife are you?"

Aaliyah's efforts were constantly undermined, and no matter how hard she tried, nothing was ever good enough. She started to doubt herself, wondering if maybe she really was as incompetent as Salma made her out to be.

Even her appearance became a source of torment. Aaliyah had always taken pride in her long, beautiful hair, but under Salma's watchful eye, her self-esteem began to erode. Salma would make offhand remarks about how Aaliyah's hair was too long and impractical, suggesting that it made her look vain. At first, Aaliyah shrugged it off, but the comments became more frequent, and soon, they began to take their toll.

One day, after a particularly harsh scolding, Aaliyah found herself in the bathroom, staring at her reflection. Her once vibrant hair, which had always been her pride, now felt like a burden. Salma's words echoed in her mind, and in a moment of weakness, Aaliyah grabbed a pair of scissors and cut off a large portion of her hair.

She regretted it immediately, tears streaming down her face as she watched her once-beautiful hair fall to the floor. But when Salma saw the result, she only smirked.

"Much better," Salma said with satisfaction. "Now you look like a proper wife. Modest and humble."

SCENE 5: THE BATHROOM Incident

The worst of Salma's cruelty came during a particularly harsh winter when Aaliyah was already feeling under the weather. It had been a long day of chores, and Aaliyah, exhausted and aching, decided to take a bath to soothe her muscles. She drew herself a hot bath, grateful for a few moments of solitude. But her peace was short-lived.

Salma burst into the bathroom without knocking, her face twisted in anger.

"How dare you waste water like this?" Salma shouted. "This is not your father's house where you can do whatever you want! We have rules here, and you will follow them!"

Aaliyah tried to cover herself, humiliated and shaken by Salma's intrusion. But Salma wasn't done. She reached over and pulled the plug, draining the bathwater right in front of Aaliyah.

"Get out," Salma ordered. "You've been pampered enough. Go clean the kitchen."

Aaliyah, shivering and drenched, climbed out of the tub, her heart pounding in her chest. She couldn't believe the level of cruelty Salma had shown. It wasn't just about control anymore—it was about humiliation, about breaking Aaliyah's spirit. And as she stood there, dripping wet and trembling, she realized that Salma would never be satisfied until she had complete dominance over her.

SCENE 6: THE SILENT Witness

Hassan, oblivious to his mother's cruelty, never questioned her behaviour. He rarely asked Aaliyah how she was doing, and when he did, it was usually in passing, as if he were fulfilling an obligation rather than genuinely caring. Aaliyah longed for him to notice, to see the torment she endured every day, but he remained blind to it all.

Hassan had two elder brothers, both married and living in America. They rarely visited, and when they did, they never stayed long. During their visits, Salma would put on a show of warmth and affection, treating Aaliyah with surprising kindness in front of her sons. It was all an act, of course, and the moment they left, the cruelty resumed.

Hassan's brothers had escaped Salma's control by moving abroad, leaving Aaliyah to bear the brunt of their mother's viciousness. Aaliyah couldn't help but wonder if they had always known what Salma was like and if that was why they had left. She envied them, wished she could escape the way they had, but she was trapped, with nowhere to turn.

SCENE 7: A MOMENT OF Despair

One night, after another day of relentless criticism and sabotage, Aaliyah found herself sitting on the edge of her bed, staring at the floor. She felt utterly defeated, her spirit crushed by the weight of Salma's cruelty. Her mind raced with thoughts of escape, of finding a way out of this nightmare, but she knew that leaving was not an option—not yet.

She thought about calling her family, but the shame of admitting her failure held her back. She had always been so strong, so confident in her ability to handle anything life threw at her. But now, she felt like a shadow of her former self, worn down by the constant abuse.

Aaliyah closed her eyes and prayed for strength. She prayed for guidance, for a way to survive in this house without losing herself completely. And as she prayed, a single tear slipped down her cheek.

"Ya Allah, "she whispered into the night. "Help me find a way through this. Grant me the strength to endure."

And with that, Aaliyah lay down, her heart heavy with despair but still clinging to the hope that someday, things would get better.

Chapter 3

The Deception Revealed

Scene 1: The Hidden Truth

The days blended into weeks, and the weight of Aaliyah's life in her in-laws' home grew heavier with each passing moment. Salma's cruelty continued unabated—each day brought a new way for her to chip away at Aaliyah's spirit. The taunts, the sabotage, the insults were relentless. Yet, Aaliyah had no choice but to endure it. She no longer found solace in the small things she used to love—cooking, cleaning, even praying had become difficult with Salma watching her every move. Every moment felt like a test she was doomed to fail.

But then came a flicker of hope—unexpected and terrifying all at once. Aaliyah began feeling faint, and waves of nausea hit her at odd times during the day. At first, she thought it was due to the stress and constant exhaustion. But after days of feeling ill, she began to suspect something more. With quiet desperation, she purchased a pregnancy test during one of her rare solo trips to the market.

When the test confirmed her suspicions, Aaliyah stared at the result in stunned silence. She was pregnant. A surge of mixed emotions hit her—joy, fear, uncertainty. A new life was growing inside her, a life that was innocent and pure, yet tied to a marriage and household that had only brought her pain. This child, her child, would be born into a world of cruelty if things didn't change.

"Ya Allah, "she whispered, her hands trembling as she held the test. "What am I supposed to do?"

Aaliyah wanted to feel happiness, but it was clouded by the reality of her situation. She couldn't bear the thought of her child growing up in this oppressive household, under the watchful eyes of Salma and the indifferent care of Hassan. She had to leave. She had to protect her child from the darkness that surrounded her. But how? How could she escape when she was so tightly controlled?

She resolved to keep the pregnancy a secret for as long as possible. If Salma or Hassan found out, they would tighten their grip on her even more, using the baby as another chain to bind her to this life of torment. She needed time to figure out a plan, to find a way out before it was too late.

SCENE 2: THE CRUMBLING Facade

As the weeks passed, Aaliyah did her best to hide her condition. She wore looser clothing, worked extra hard to mask her fatigue, and pretended that everything was fine. Every night, as she lay in bed, she whispered prayers for her unborn child, asking Allah for guidance and protection.

But as her pregnancy progressed, it became harder to conceal. She began to feel weak, struggling to complete the endless chores Salma assigned her. The nausea was constant, and there were days when she could barely keep her food down. Still, she persisted, knowing that her child's future depended on her ability to escape this house.

Salma noticed the changes in Aaliyah's behaviour but dismissed them as signs of laziness. She took every opportunity to berate Aaliyah for her perceived incompetence, belittling her at every turn.

"You're getting even more useless by the day," Salma sneered one morning as Aaliyah struggled to clean the kitchen. *"What did my son ever see in you? If you can't even keep up with simple tasks, how do you expect to be a good wife?"

Aaliyah bit her tongue, swallowing the anger and frustration that threatened to spill over. She couldn't afford to lose control now—not when she was so close to finding a way out. She clung to the thought of her child, to the hope that she could leave this house and give her baby a better life.

SCENE 3: THE UNEXPECTED Visit

One afternoon, as Aaliyah was going about her routine, she heard voices at the front door—familiar voices that made her heart leap with both joy and fear. Her parents had come to visit. They had not seen her for months, and she had not been able to call them without Salma monitoring every word. They were undoubtedly worried about her and had decided to visit unannounced.

Aaliyah quickly rushed to the entrance, wiping her hands on her apron as she prepared herself to greet them. Her parents stood at the door, smiling warmly, but there was concern in their eyes as they took in her appearance. Aaliyah's mother, Amina, immediately noticed the dark circles under her daughter's eyes, the thinness of her frame, and the tension that seemed to radiate from her.

"Aaliyah," her mother said gently, taking her hands, "we've missed you so much. Are you alright?"

Aaliyah forced a smile, trying to hide her true emotions. She felt a lump form in her throat, the desire to throw herself into her mother's arms overwhelming her. But she couldn't let her parents see the full extent of her pain—not yet.

"I'm fine, Mama," Aaliyah replied softly, her voice shaky. "It's just... things have been busy here."

Salma appeared at that moment, her face stretched into a tight, fake smile as she greeted Aaliyah's parents. She ushered them inside with a politeness that Aaliyah knew was insincere. Aaliyah's father, Yusuf, exchanged pleasantries with Salma, but Aaliyah could see that her parents were uneasy.

"Why didn't you tell us you were coming? "Salma asked in a tone that suggested she would have found a way to stop them if she had known. "It's such a surprise!"

"We just wanted to see our daughter," Yusuf said. "It's been a long time, and we've missed her."

Salma's smile tightened even further, and Aaliyah could feel the tension in the air. She could only hope that her parents wouldn't ask too many questions—questions she couldn't answer honestly while Salma and Hassan were around.

SCENE 4: THE CONFRONTATION

As they sat in the living room, sipping tea and making small talk, Aaliyah's mother couldn't contain her concern any longer. She leaned forward and placed a hand on Aaliyah's arm, her voice low and gentle.

"Aaliyah, are you sure everything is alright?" Amina asked softly. "You look tired, and you've lost so much weight. Please, if something is wrong, you can tell us."

Aaliyah's heart raced. She glanced at Salma, who was watching her closely, her eyes cold and calculating. Aaliyah knew she had to tread carefully. She couldn't reveal the truth—not with Salma sitting right there.

"I'm just adjusting, Mama," Aaliyah said, forcing another smile. "It's a big change, but I'm managing."

Amina didn't look convinced, and neither did Yusuf. They exchanged a worried glance, and Yusuf cleared his throat before speaking.

"Aaliyah," he said gently, "if you ever need anything—if you ever need to come home—you know our doors are always open. You don't have to stay here if things aren't right."

Aaliyah felt tears prick at the corners of her eyes. She wanted nothing more than to cry out, to beg them to take her away from this place. But she knew that if she did, Salma and Hassan would make her life even more unbearable. And now, with a baby on the way, the stakes were even higher.

Salma interrupted before Aaliyah could respond, her voice dripping with false sweetness.

"Aaliyah is perfectly fine here," she said. "She's just been adjusting to her new role as a wife. It's natural for there to be a few challenges at first, but she's doing well."

Amina looked at Salma with a mixture of suspicion and frustration, but she didn't press the issue further. She knew there was more going on than Aaliyah was letting on, but she also understood that this was not the time or place for a confrontation.

"If you say so, "Amina replied, her voice tight.

The visit continued with forced pleasantries, but the tension in the room was palpable. Aaliyah's parents stayed for a few more hours, but when they finally left, they hugged Aaliyah tightly, whispering words of love and support into her ear.

"We're always here for you, Aaliyah," her mother whispered. "Always."

Aaliyah nodded, fighting back tears as she watched them leave. The moment the door closed behind them, Salma's kind façade disappeared. She turned to Aaliyah with a scowl, her eyes narrowing.

"Don't think for a second that I didn't see what you were trying to do," Salma hissed. "You may have fooled your parents, but you can't fool me. You're not going anywhere."

Aaliyah's heart sank. Salma's words confirmed her worst fears—Salma would do everything in her power to keep Aaliyah trapped in this house, no matter what. And with the baby growing inside her, Aaliyah knew she had even less time than she thought to find a way out.

SCENE 5: A DESPERATE Plan

That night, as Aaliyah lay in bed, her mind raced with thoughts of escape. She couldn't stay here much longer—Salma's cruelty was growing more intense by the day, and with the pregnancy progressing, it would soon become impossible to hide. She couldn't risk her child growing up in this environment, under the control of a woman as heartless as Salma and a husband as indifferent as Hassan.

She knew she needed a plan—a way to leave without raising suspicion, without alerting Salma or Hassan to her intentions. But how? Salma monitored her every move, and Hassan rarely paid attention to her beyond making sure she fulfilled her duties as a wife. The window for escape was small, but it was there, and Aaliyah was determined to find it.

"Ya Allah," she prayed that night, her hands resting on her still-flat stomach. "Give me the strength to protect this child. Help me find a way to break free from this prison."

As she drifted off to sleep, her mind began to form a plan—a desperate plan, but one that just might work. She would have to be careful, patient, and clever, but if she succeeded, she could finally be free. She would have a chance at a new life for herself and her child, away from the cruelty of Salma and the indifference of Hassan.

And so, with renewed determination, Aaliyah began to prepare for the next phase of her life—a life of freedom and hope, far from the torment that had plagued her for so long.

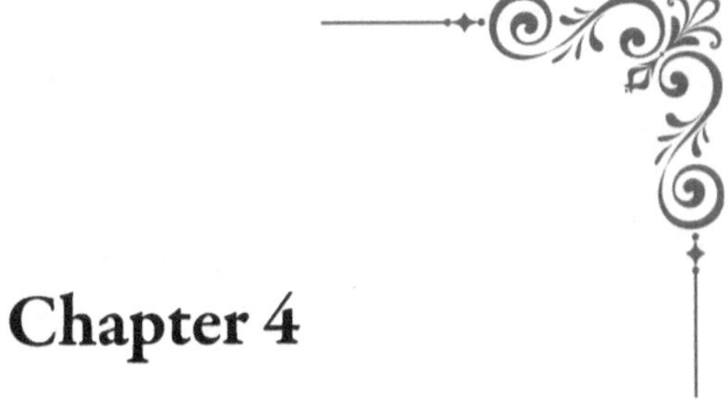

Chapter 4

The Breaking Point

Scene 1: The Family Function

A few months had passed since Aaliyah discovered her pregnancy, and every day since then had been a delicate balancing act. She had kept the secret hidden, but it was getting harder to conceal the changes in her body. She wore looser clothes and moved cautiously, avoiding attention as much as possible, all while trying to avoid Salma's sharp gaze. But despite her best efforts, the toll of stress and isolation was wearing her down.

One afternoon, Hassan's family organized a large gathering—a celebration of an extended relative's engagement. The house was buzzing with activity. Guests filled the living room, and the scent of food wafted from the kitchen. Salma, as always, barked orders at Aaliyah, demanding that she help with the preparations and serve the guests. Though Aaliyah was exhausted and her body ached, she did her best to keep up.

Amidst the commotion, Aaliyah saw her chance to escape unnoticed. She had been experiencing sharp pains in her abdomen for days, and she needed to see a doctor. She had managed to arrange a secret appointment at a clinic not far from the house. Slipping out during the height of the celebration, she quietly excused herself, telling Salma that she needed to fetch more supplies for the function.

Salma barely glanced at her, too busy with her guests to pay much attention. It was the opening Aaliyah had been waiting for.

SCENE 2: THE SECRET Doctor's Visit

Aliya rushed to the clinic, her heart pounding with both fear and anticipation. When she arrived, the waiting room was empty, and the nurse led her to the examination room without delay. The doctor, a kind older woman, asked Aliya to describe her symptoms and how far along she believed she was in her pregnancy.

"I've kept it a secret from my family," Aliya explained, her voice trembling. "They don't know. My mother-in-law... she controls everything. I haven't been able to see a doctor until now."

The doctor listened carefully, her expression softening with understanding. After conducting an ultrasound, she turned to Aliya with a reassuring smile.

"You're about five months along," the doctor said gently. "Everything seems to be fine with the baby, but you need to take better care of yourself. You're underweight, and the stress is affecting your health. You'll need regular check-up's from here on."

Aliya sighed in relief, though the weight of her situation pressed down harder than ever. She thanked the doctor and left the clinic, knowing she would have to continue hiding her condition until she could find a way out of the house. Time was running out, and her pregnancy could no longer be kept secret for much longer.

As Aaliyah walked back toward Hassan's home, she rehearsed her excuse in her head, preparing to explain her absence as though it were nothing out of the ordinary. She hoped the commotion of the function would provide enough cover for her to slip back in without anyone noticing she had been gone.

SCENE 3: THE BETRAYAL

Aaliyah's hope of sneaking back into the house unnoticed was quickly dashed. The moment she stepped inside, Salma was waiting for her, a furious look in her eyes. Aaliyah's heart sank—Salma must have noticed her absence after all.

"Where have you been?" Salma demanded, her voice low but dripping with venom.

"I went to get some supplies for the function," Aaliyah replied nervously, trying to keep her voice steady.

But Salma wasn't fooled. She stepped closer, her eyes narrowing.

"Don't lie to me, "she hissed. "I know where you've been. You think you can sneak around behind my back? What were you doing at the clinic?"

Aaliyah's blood ran cold. How had Salma found out? Had someone seen her and reported back to Salma? Panic surged through her veins as she searched for words, but before she could respond, Salma grabbed her arm roughly.

"Hassan!" Salma called out, her voice sharp and commanding.

Hassan entered the room, his expression darkening when he saw the scene unfolding before him. Salma wasted no time in spinning her web of lies, twisting the situation to her advantage.

"Your wife has been sneaking off behind our backs," Salma said, her voice filled with false concern. "I caught her sneaking back into the house after a secret visit to the doctor. Who knows what she's been doing, but she's been hiding something from us. She's making a fool of you."

Hassan's eyes flared with anger. He turned to Aaliyah, his fists clenched at his sides.

"Is this true?" he demanded. "What have you been hiding?"

Aaliyah tried to explain, to tell him the truth, but the words wouldn't come. She was too frightened, too overwhelmed by the intensity of the situation. All she could do was shake her head, her eyes pleading for understanding.

But Hassan's anger had already boiled over. He grabbed Aaliyah by the shoulders and shoved her against the wall, his eyes burning with rage.

"You've disgraced me," he growled. "You've been lying to me this whole time!"

Before Aliya could react, Hassan struck her hard across the face, sending her crashing to the floor. The room spun as she hit the ground, pain radiating through her body. She gasped for breath, clutching her stomach in fear for her baby.

Salma stood by, her face devoid of emotion as she watched the scene unfold. She made no attempt to stop Hassan, instead fuelling his anger with her accusations.

"She's not fit to be your wife," Salma said coldly. "She's been nothing but a burden to this family."

Aaliyah's vision blurred as she struggled to stay conscious. She could hear Hassan's voice above her, shouting words she couldn't fully comprehend. Her body felt heavy, and she couldn't fight the darkness closing in around her. The last thing she remembered was the feeling of helplessness washing over her before she slipped into unconsciousness.

SCENE 4: THE SECRET Doctor

When Aaliyah awoke, she found herself lying in bed, the soft glow of a lamp casting shadows on the walls. Her head throbbed, and her body ached from the beating she had endured. She could hear voices nearby—low, urgent voices speaking in hushed tones.

Slowly, she turned her head and saw Hassan and Salma standing by the door, speaking to a man she didn't recognize. The man was dressed in a simple doctor's coat, and he held a medical bag in his hands.

"We don't want this getting out," Salma was saying. "You'll come through the back door next time, and you'll keep this visit quiet. Understood?"

The doctor nodded, his expression serious. He glanced over at Aaliyah, then back at Salma.

"She's pregnant," the doctor said quietly. "About five months along. I'm surprised she didn't tell you sooner."

Hassan's face contorted in shock. He turned to Aaliyah, disbelief written across his features.

"Five months?" Hassan repeated, his voice rising with incredulity. *"How could she be five months pregnant and not say a word?"

Salma quickly stepped in, her mind racing to cover up her earlier lies.

"Well, Hassan," she said, her tone smooth, "you've been married for nearly eight months. Time has flown by so quickly, hasn't it? Maybe she didn't even realize it herself. You know how these things can happen."

Hassan still looked confused, but the doctor's presence seemed to calm him somewhat. He glanced at Aliya with a mixture of anger and bewilderment, but he said nothing more. The doctor began to examine Aliya, checking her vital signs and assessing the damage from the beating.

"She's stable," the doctor said after a few minutes. "But she needs rest. The stress and the trauma she's been through are dangerous for both her and the baby. You need to make sure she takes it easy from now on."

Salma gave a curt nod, though Aaliyah knew that her mother-in-law had no intention of making her life easier. This was all about appearances—Salma would do whatever was necessary to maintain the family's image, but she had no real concern for Aaliyah's well-being.

The doctor packed up his bag and left through the back door, just as Salma had instructed. Once he was gone, Hassan sat down on the edge of the bed, his expression unreadable.

"Why didn't you tell me?" he asked quietly, though the anger still simmered beneath his words.

Aaliyah's throat felt dry, and it was difficult to speak, but she forced the words out.

"I was afraid," she whispered. "I was afraid of what you and your mother would do."

Hassan frowned, but he said nothing in response. He stood up and walked toward the door, leaving Aaliyah alone in the room. Salma stayed behind for a moment, her cold gaze lingering on Aaliyah.

"You've caused enough trouble," Salma said softly. "But don't worry. We'll take care of everything from now on."

And with that, Salma left the room, closing the door behind her.

SCENE 5: A MOMENT OF Reflection

As the days passed, Aaliyah remained confined to her bed, her body slowly recovering from the trauma. She felt weak and helpless, trapped in a situation that seemed increasingly hopeless. Salma and Hassan kept their distance, but Aaliyah could feel their presence lurking around every corner. They were watching her, waiting for her next move.

Aaliyah's thoughts were consumed by her baby—her child, who was growing inside her despite the darkness that surrounded them both. She knew that she had to protect this child at all costs, but how? How could she protect her baby when she couldn't even protect herself?

Her resolve began to harden. She couldn't continue living like this. She couldn't allow her child to be born into a world of fear and cruelty. She needed to find a way out—no matter what it took.

"Ya Allah," she prayed silently, her hands resting on her belly. "Grant me the strength to leave this place. Help me protect my child."

Aaliyah knew that the road ahead would be difficult, but she was determined to escape. She had to. For herself, for her baby, and for the future they both deserved.

Chapter 5

The Path of Healing

Scene 1: A Mother's Hope

Aaliyah held her new born son close to her chest, the rhythmic beating of his tiny heart against hers offering the only comfort in a life that had become increasingly unbearable. After months of torment and cruelty, the birth of her son was the one glimmer of hope she had left. She named him Adnan, a name that carried strength, hoping that her child would be resilient in a world so harsh and unforgiving.

For a short while after Adnan's birth, things seemed to improve. Hassan, once cold and indifferent, had softened toward her, if only slightly. He would watch as Aaliyah held their baby, his eyes distant yet softer than they had been before. Sometimes, he would sit beside her and brush his hand over the baby's head, whispering that maybe now their family could find peace. In those rare moments, Aaliyah clung to the hope that motherhood would change things, that maybe Hassan's heart could finally open.

But deep down, she knew better. The shadow of Salma lingered, dark and malevolent, and the fear of her wrath never left Aaliyah's heart. Salma was terrified that Aaliyah would do what Hassan's brothers' wives had done—take her son away from her and move to a different country. The thought consumed her, and she watched Aaliyah like a hawk, waiting for any sign of disobedience.

"Don't think for a second that I don't see what you're trying to do," Salma whispered one night as Aaliyah rocked Adnan to sleep. "I won't let you take Hassan away from me like the others did. I've already seen it happen with my other sons. You'll destroy him, and I'll stop at nothing to make sure that doesn't happen."

Aaliyah shuddered at her words, clutching Adnan tighter. She couldn't imagine leaving without her son, but the fear of Salma's retaliation made her hesitate. She had no money, no phone, no way to contact her family. Salma had stripped her of everything, even taking the jewellery Aaliyah's parents had gifted her on her wedding day. She was a prisoner in this house, and every day the walls seemed to close in on her a little more.

— ⟲ —

SCENE 2: SALMA'S POISON

As time went by, Salma became more devious, setting traps in her relentless campaign to tear Aaliyah down. She began spreading rumours within the family that Aaliyah was having an affair with her cousin. The accusations came out of nowhere—Aaliyah hadn't seen her cousin in over a year, and the last time they had spoken was briefly at her wedding. Nevertheless, Salma twisted reality, manipulating Hassan into believing that Aaliyah's loyalty was questionable.

"She's been sneaking around," Salma would tell Hassan in a hushed tone when Aaliyah wasn't in the room. "She's been meeting with her cousin behind your back. You think she's pure, but I've seen the way she acts when you're not around. Don't let her fool you."

Hassan, already insecure and easily swayed by his mother, began to believe Salma's lies. The doubt crept into his heart, poisoning the fragile connection he had started to rebuild with Aaliyah after Adnan's birth. He became suspicious of every word Aaliyah said, every glance she cast, even though Aaliyah was innocent.

One night, Hassan confronted her with accusations that took Aaliyah completely by surprise.

"Do you think I'm a fool?";Hassan spat as Aaliyah tried to nurse Adnan. "I know what you're doing. You've been meeting with your cousin, haven't you? How long has this been going on?"

Aaliyah was stunned, her mind racing to comprehend the accusations. She hadn't seen her cousin in over a year, and the suggestion of an affair was so far from the truth that she didn't know how to respond.

"I don't understand what you're saying," Aaliyah whispered, tears welling up in her eyes. "I haven't seen my cousin since the wedding. I swear, I've done nothing wrong."

But Hassan wasn't listening. His anger had already taken root, fuelled by his mother's lies. He pushed Aaliyah roughly to the floor, shouting insults that pierced her heart like daggers.

"You're a liar!" he screamed. "You think you can fool me, but I know what you're doing. You're trying to make me look like a fool. But I won't let you. You're mine. You belong to me, not to some other man!"

Aaliyah, still holding Adnan, tried to shield her baby from Hassan's outburst. But there was no protection from the verbal and physical abuse that followed. Hassan hit her, pushed her, and accused her of being unfaithful, all while Adnan cried in her arms.

"Come to bed, now," Hassan demanded later that night. "Or are you thinking about running away with some other man?"

Aaliyah froze. She had just managed to put Adnan to sleep, and her body ached from Hassan's earlier assault. She wanted nothing more than to stay by her son's side, but Hassan's words left her no choice. When she hesitated, he grabbed her roughly, forcing her onto the bed.

"I have rights over you," Hassan growled. "You're my wife, and you'll do as I say."

Despite her pleas, Hassan ignored her cries and raped her that night. Aaliyah felt trapped in her own skin, suffocated by the man who was supposed to be her protector, but who had become her oppressor. Tears streamed down her face as Hassan violated her again and again, the pain of his cruelty eclipsing everything else.

She whispered prayers in the darkness, pleading with Allah for an escape, but the only sound that came in response was Adnan's quiet cries from the crib nearby.

SCENE 3: STRIPPED OF Freedom

In the following months, Salma tightened her grip on Aaliyah's life even further. She took away Aaliyah's last remaining possessions—her phone, her jewellery, and any means of contacting her family. Salma had already isolated her from the outside world, but now, she made sure that Aaliyah had no way of escaping or telling anyone about the abuse she was enduring.

"You'll stay in this house," Salma said coldly as she snatched the phone from Aaliyah's hand. "You'll do what you're told, and you won't speak to your family again. You have everything you need right here. Don't think for a second that you can run away."

Aaliyah was trapped, with no one to turn to and no way to reach out for help. The days blurred into one another, filled with endless chores, emotional torment, and the constant fear of Hassan's unpredictable anger. She became a shadow of her former self, her body frail and her spirit broken. Adnan, her only light in the darkness, gave her the strength to keep going, but even that strength was beginning to fade.

Salma watched Aaliyah like a predator, waiting for any sign of weakness. And when Aaliyah did falter—when the exhaustion became too much and she could barely stand on her feet—Salma pounced, taking every opportunity to humiliate her in front of Hassan and anyone else who was present.

"Look at her," Salma would say with disdain. She's weak, lazy. She doesn't deserve you, Hassan. She's trying to play the victim, but I see through her lies. She's not fit to be a wife or a mother."

Hassan, blinded by his mother's manipulation, believed every word she said. His moments of sympathy for Aaliyah had vanished, replaced by anger, suspicion, and cruelty. He began hitting her more frequently, sometimes for no reason at all. And each time, Aaliyah retreated further into herself, hiding her pain from everyone around her.

SCENE 4: THE COUSIN'S Visit

Five months after Adnan's birth, Hassan's cousin and his family came to visit. It was supposed to be a joyous occasion—an opportunity for the family to see Adnan and celebrate the birth of a new member of the family. But for Aaliyah, the visit was anything but joyful.

She was exhausted, her body and mind worn down by the abuse and the relentless demands of her daily life. She greeted the guests as best she could, offering them tea and trying to hide the strain she was under. But her hands trembled, and her eyes were heavy with fatigue.

Salma noticed immediately. She watched Aaliyah closely, her eyes narrowing with suspicion. When Aaliyah excused herself to take a short break and rest, Salma made sure to manipulate the situation, making herself appear as the caring mother-in-law.

"Hassan," Salma said sweetly, "why don't you take Aaliyah to the bedroom to rest? She's exhausted, poor thing."

Hassan, playing the part of the caring husband in front of the guests, nodded and led Aaliyah to the bedroom. But as soon as the door was closed behind them, his demeanour shifted.

Aaliyah collapsed onto the bed, her body shaking with nausea. She felt sick to her stomach, and before she could stop herself, she vomited on the floor. Hassan recoiled in disgust.

"What's wrong with you?" he snapped, his voice filled with anger. "You can't even control yourself!"

Aaliyah tried to apologize, but before she could speak, Hassan's anger boiled over. His eyes burned with fury as he grabbed her by the arm, yanking her off the bed. She barely had time to react before he shoved her against the wall, his face inches from hers.

"You disgust me," he spat. "You think you're so clever, playing the innocent wife in front of the guests. But I know the truth. You're weak, pathetic."

Aaliyah felt her body tremble with fear. Her head was spinning, and the sickness she had been battling for days seemed to worsen in that moment. She reached for the wall to steady herself, but Hassan grabbed her again, this time with more force.

Without warning, he locked the bedroom door and windows, sealing them both inside. His rage had reached a point where there was no reasoning with him. He wasn't just angry—he was out for blood. Aaliyah's heart raced as panic set in.

"Please," she begged, her voice barely a whisper. "Please, Hassan, I'm sorry. I didn't mean to—"

But Hassan wasn't listening. He grabbed a towel from the nearby dresser and shoved it into her mouth, gagging her. Aaliyah's eyes filled with tears as she struggled to breathe, fear gripping her chest. Her body was too weak to resist, too fragile from months of abuse, stress, and exhaustion.

Then the blows began.

Hassan hit her again and again, his fists landing on her arms, her stomach, her back. The pain was excruciating, and with every hit, Aaliyah felt her strength slipping away. She tried to scream, but the towel muffled her cries. She wanted to protect herself, but she had no energy left to fight.

Finally, after what felt like an eternity, Hassan stopped. He stood over her, breathing heavily, his face twisted with anger. Aaliyah lay on the floor, curled into a ball, barely conscious. Her vision was blurred, her body aching in ways she had never known. She felt herself slipping into unconsciousness, her mind going numb to the pain.

Just as darkness began to overtake her, she heard a faint sound—someone knocking on the door. It was distant, almost like a dream, but it was real. Someone was outside, and they had heard the commotion.

The door swung open, and through her hazy vision, Aaliyah saw Leena, Hassan's cousin's daughter, standing in the doorway. Leena's eyes widened in shock as she took in the scene—the vomit on the floor, the broken woman lying on the ground, and the blood on Hassan's knuckles.

"What have you done?" Leena whispered, her voice trembling. "Hassan, what have you done?"

Hassan, caught off guard, glared at Leena, his anger still simmering beneath the surface. But the presence of a witness seemed to cool his rage momentarily. Without a word, he stormed out of the room, leaving the door wide open. The sound of his footsteps echoed down the hallway as he made his way to his office, slamming the door behind him.

Leena rushed to Aaliyah's side, her face filled with concern. She knelt down beside her, gently lifting her into a sitting position. Aaliyah winced as pain shot through her body, but she was too weak to resist Leena's help.

"It's okay, Aaliyah," Leena whispered. "I'm here. Let me help you."

Leena fetched some water and a damp cloth from the adjoining bathroom. She cleaned Aaliyah's wounds as best she could, her hands shaking with every touch. Aaliyah could see the fear in Leena's eyes, but there was also a deep sense of compassion.

"I've known Hassan my whole life," Leena said quietly as she tended to Aaliyah's injuries. "He's always had a temper, but this... this is torture. No one deserves this."

Aaliyah forced a weak smile, her voice barely a whisper.

"Jazakallahu khair," she said in Arabic, thanking Leena for her kindness.

Leena returned the smile, though it was tinged with sadness. She helped Aaliyah back onto the bed, arranging the pillows so that she could rest more comfortably. As she worked, she spoke softly, her voice filled with emotion.

"If you ever need help," Leena said, "please let me know. I know it's hard, but you don't have to go through this alone. I'll be here for you."

Aaliyah nodded weakly, though she knew that asking for help would be nearly impossible under Salma's watchful eye. She appreciated Leena's offer, but deep down, she felt trapped. The abuse, the lies, the isolation—there seemed to be no way out.

Just then, Salma called for Leena from downstairs. Leena hesitated, glancing toward the door with a look of concern, but Aaliyah nodded, urging her to go. Leena left reluctantly, casting one last worried glance at Aaliyah before disappearing down the stairs.

SCENE 5: THE AFTERMATH

The days that followed were a blur for Aaliyah. Her body was battered, her spirit broken, and her hope for escape seemed to dwindle with every passing moment. She remained bedridden for days, her body too weak to move, while Salma and Hassan continued their charade of normalcy for the rest of the family.

Salma was careful to keep the truth hidden. She insisted that Aaliyah had come down with a terrible illness, fabricating a story to explain her absence from family gatherings and social events. She told everyone that Aaliyah was too weak to come downstairs, keeping visitors away so that no one would see the bruises and scars that marred Aaliyah's once-beautiful skin.

But the pain wasn't just physical. Aaliyah's heart was shattered. She had once hoped that motherhood would bring change, that perhaps Hassan's cruelty would lessen with the birth of their son. But Adnan's presence had only seemed to make things worse. Salma's jealousy, Hassan's suspicion—it had all reached a boiling point, and Aaliyah felt powerless to stop it.

Every night, Aaliyah lay awake in the dark, her mind racing with thoughts of escape. She couldn't stay in this house forever, not with the constant threat of violence hanging over her head. But how could she leave? Salma had taken everything—her phone, her money, her freedom. And now, with Adnan's safety on the line, she couldn't risk leaving without a plan.

Aaliyah whispered silent prayers into the night, asking Allah for guidance and strength. She knew that she had to find a way to break free, not just for herself, but for her son. Adnan deserved a life free from fear and violence, and Aaliyah was determined to give him that, even if it meant risking everything.

SCENE 6: A GLIMMER of Hope

RESILIENCE IN THE SHADOWS

As Aaliyah's strength slowly returned, so did her resolve. She began to notice small cracks in the fortress that Salma had built around her. Leena continued to visit occasionally, always finding ways to slip Aaliyah small bits of help—medication for her wounds, a sympathetic ear, and even the occasional kind word of encouragement.

Aaliyah was grateful for Leena's support, but she knew she couldn't rely on her cousin's daughter alone. She had to take matters into her own hands if she ever hoped to escape. With every passing day, she gathered what little strength she had left, planning her next steps carefully. She couldn't afford any mistakes.

One evening, as the house quieted and Salma and Hassan retreated to their respective rooms, Aaliyah quietly got out of bed. She moved slowly, her body still sore from the beating, but her determination fuelled her. She crept down the hallway toward the study, where Hassan kept his phone and wallet.

She knew that if she could just get her hands on the phone, she might be able to contact her family. Her parents had no idea what was happening to her—they had been kept in the dark by Salma's lies. If she could reach them, perhaps they could help her escape this nightmare once and for all.

Her heart raced as she approached the study door. She carefully turned the knob, praying that it wouldn't make a sound. The door creaked open, and Aaliyah slipped inside. She scanned the room quickly, searching for the phone. It sat on the desk, just within reach.

With trembling hands, Aaliyah grabbed the phone and quickly dialled her parents' number. The phone rang once, twice, and then—

"Hello?" her mother's voice answered on the other end of the line.

Tears filled Aaliyah's eyes as she heard the familiar voice of her mother. She opened her mouth to speak, but just as she was about to say something, she heard footsteps approaching the study. Panic surged through her veins as she quickly hung up the phone and placed it back on the desk.

She had been so close—so close to finally reaching out for help. But now, with Salma or Hassan on the way, she had no choice but to retreat back to her room. She would have to try again another night, but at least now she knew that her parents were just a phone call away.

With renewed determination, Aaliyah slipped out of the study and back into her bedroom. She knew that escaping would not be easy, but she had taken the first step. She would find a way out of this house, no matter how long it took.

For the first time in months, Aaliyah allowed herself a small glimmer of hope. The path to healing was long and treacherous, but she had taken the first step toward freedom. And for the sake of her son, she would keep fighting until the day she could finally leave this nightmare behind.

Chapter 6

The Path to Freedom

Scene 1: A Mother's Intuition

The morning sunlight filtered through the curtains, casting a warm glow over the breakfast table. But Amina's heart was far from feeling light. She sat at the head of the table, her hands wrapped around her cup of tea, staring into the swirling liquid as a sense of unease gripped her chest.

It had been months since she had heard from Aaliyah. The last time they had visited her daughter's home, everything had seemed fine—Hassan and his family had been polite, and Aaliyah had appeared to be in good hands. But lately, something felt wrong. Last night, an unknown number had called her phone. She hadn't picked up in time, and there had been no voicemail, but deep in her heart, Amina felt certain that it had been Aaliyah trying to reach out to her. She couldn't shake the feeling of foreboding, and it had kept her awake for most of the night.

"I don't know, Yusuf, "she said quietly, breaking the silence. "Something is wrong. I feel it in my bones. Aaliyah hasn't called us in so long. What if she's in trouble?"

Yusuf, who had been reading the newspaper, looked up at his wife with a reassuring smile.

"Don't worry so much, Amina," he said softly. "Our daughter is in good hands. Remember how well they treated her the last time we visited? I'm sure she's just busy with the baby. She'll call us soon."

But Amina couldn't find comfort in his words. She pushed her plate of food away, unable to eat. Her appetite had vanished, replaced by the gnawing worry for her daughter.

"I think we should visit her," Amina insisted. "I just want to make sure she's alright."

Yusuf sighed, glancing at the clock. He had a busy day ahead with important meetings at the company, and the thought of delaying them didn't sit well with him.

"I can't today, Amina, "he said, trying to remain patient. "I have back-to-back meetings, and it's not easy to reschedule. Trust me, Aaliyah is fine."

Amina was about to argue when their younger son, Mohammad, interrupted. He had been listening quietly to the conversation, sensing his mother's distress. Now, he looked up from his plate and spoke with determination.

"I'll go check on her, Mama," Mohammad said. "I'll visit Aaliyah and make sure she's okay. Safiya can come with me—she's been wanting to see the baby anyway."

Safiya, Aaliyah's younger sister, smiled brightly at the suggestion.

"Yes! I would love to see little Adnan again. He's so adorable!" she exclaimed, her face lighting up.

Amina's heart swelled with gratitude. She nodded, feeling a sense of relief wash over her.

"Thank you, my dears, "Amina said, her voice softer now. "I'll pack some of Aaliyah's favourites snacks for you to take with you."

While Amina busied herself in the kitchen, preparing a small box of treats, she couldn't help but pray silently.

"Ya Allah, she thought, protect my daughter and keep her safe."

SCENE 2: A DESPERATE Reunion

Aaliyah sat in the dimly lit living room, her body weak and fragile from months of abuse. The bruises on her arms and legs had faded to a sickly yellow, but the pain remained. She had grown thinner, and her once-vibrant face now looked gaunt and hollow. Every day felt like a battle to survive, and her spirit had been all but crushed beneath Salma and Hassan's cruelty.

Salma continued to monitor her every move, her sharp eyes always watching for any signs of rebellion. Aaliyah was not allowed to leave the house, not even to go outside for fresh air. Her phone had been confiscated, her jewellery taken away, and any contact with the outside world was strictly forbidden.

As Aaliyah sat in the living room that afternoon, trying to feed Adnan with trembling hands, she heard Hassan's voice on the phone with Salma. He was calling to say that he wouldn't be home for dinner, as work would keep him away until the next morning.

"Take care of Adnan for me, Mother," Hassan instructed before hanging up.

Salma relayed the message to Aaliyah with her usual cold indifference. "Hassan won't be home tonight," she said. "Don't cause any trouble."

Aaliyah nodded quietly, her heart sinking further into despair. She didn't have the energy to argue, let alone resist. She just wanted the day to pass without incident, to survive until tomorrow.

Then, the doorbell rang.

Salma stood up from her chair, a look of confusion crossing her face. They weren't expecting any visitors. She walked to the front door and opened it, only to find Mohammad and Safiya standing on the doorstep, smiling warmly.

Aaliyah's heart skipped a beat as she saw her siblings standing there. For a moment, it felt as though the dark clouds that had been hovering over her had parted, allowing a sliver of sunlight to break through. She couldn't believe they were here—her brother and sister, her lifelines.

Salma's confusion deepened, but she forced a tight smile and gestured for them to come inside.

"You're here to see the baby, I suppose," Salma said curtly. "Well, don't stay too long. Aaliyah isn't feeling well."

As Salma led them into the living room, Aaliyah's eyes met Mohammad's, and in that moment, they communicated without words. There was no need to speak openly about the abuse or the pain she was enduring—they had been raised together, and their bond was strong enough that a simple glance could convey what words could not.

Mohammad sat beside Aaliyah on the sofa, his eyes searching her face for signs of distress. He noticed the bruises on her wrists, the thinness of her frame, and the exhaustion that seemed to weigh her down. Safiya, meanwhile, took the baby into her arms, cooing softly as she played with him.

Salma hovered nearby, her sharp gaze flicking between the siblings like a hawk. She was suspicious, but she didn't dare interfere too much while Mohammad and Safiya were there. They were, after all, family, and Salma didn't want to raise any alarms by acting out of character.

But Aaliyah saw this as her chance. With Salma distracted by Safiya's playful interactions with the baby, Aaliyah turned her eyes to Mohammad and communicated in Morse code, using subtle blinks and movements that only he would understand. She spelled out a message of desperation, telling him everything she couldn't say aloud.

"Help me," her blinks said. "Get me out of here."

Mohammad's eyes widened slightly as he deciphered the code. His heart ached for his sister, and he knew that he couldn't leave her in this house any longer. He needed to act, and quickly.

SCENE 3: THE PLAN FOR Escape

Mohammad excused himself, telling Salma that he needed to make a quick phone call. He stepped outside the house, his heart racing as he dialled their father's number.

"Baba, it's Mohammad," he said urgently. "Something's wrong with Aaliyah. She's in danger, and we need to get her out of that house. I'm calling the police. Please meet me there as soon as you can."

Yusuf's voice was filled with concern on the other end of the line.

"I'll be there right away," Yusuf said. "Do whatever you need to do. I'll take care of everything."

After making the call, Mohammad quickly contacted the police, explaining the situation and requesting immediate assistance. Once he had made all the necessary calls, he returned to the house, his face calm despite the storm raging inside him.

When he re-entered the living room, he told Safiya that they needed to leave, using a vague excuse about an urgent matter they had to attend to. Safiya, understanding the gravity of the situation, gently handed the baby back to Aaliyah and stood up to leave.

"We'll come back to visit again soon," Mohammad said casually, giving Salma a polite smile.

But as they walked toward the door, the doorbell rang again, and this time, when Salma opened it, she was met with the sight of the police standing on her doorstep, along with Yusuf.

Salma's heart raced, her mind struggling to make sense of what was happening. She shot a frantic look at Aaliyah, but Aaliyah stood still, her gaze steady and unwavering.

"What's going on? "Salma demanded, her voice sharp.

The police officer stepped forward, speaking firmly but respectfully.

"We've received a report of domestic abuse," the officer said. "We need to speak with Aaliyah."

Salma's face went pale, and her heart pounded in her chest. She had thought she had complete control over Aaliyah, but now everything was unravelling. How had Aaliyah managed to call for help? Salma's mind raced with questions, but none of them mattered now. The police were here, and they were going to take Aaliyah away.

SCENE 4: FREEDOM AT Last

As the police questioned Salma and Hassan's absence was noted, Yusuf rushed into the house, embracing his daughter tightly. Tears welled in Aaliyah's eyes as she clung to her father, the weight of her suffering finally lifting from her shoulders.

"Baba…" Aaliyah whispered, her voice breaking. "Please, take me home. I can't stay here anymore."

Yusuf nodded, his voice filled with determination.

"You're coming home with us, Aaliyah," he said. "No one will ever hurt you again."

With the police escorting them, Aaliyah gathered her belongings and her son, Adnan. Salma watched helplessly as Aaliyah walked out of the house, free at last. The once-proud matriarch was now left with nothing but her own bitterness and anger, her grip on Hassan slipping away just as it had with her other sons.

As Aaliyah stepped out of the house and into the sunlight, she felt a sense of relief wash over her. The nightmare was over. She was finally free.

SCENE 5: THE HEALING Begins

Back home with her family, Aaliyah began the long process of healing. She was surrounded by love and support, her family tending to her every need and making sure she was never alone. Her mother, Amina, fussed over her like she had when Aaliyah was a child, and her siblings took turns helping her care for Adnan.

Aaliyah's health began to improve, and as the weeks passed, she started to regain her strength. But the emotional scars of the abuse still haunted her. She was plagued by nightmares and flashbacks, waking in the middle of the night drenched in sweat, her heart pounding in fear. She often found herself locking the doors and windows, afraid that Hassan or Salma might somehow find her and drag her back to that house.

The doctors diagnosed her with a skin condition exacerbated by stress and neglect, but there was hope for recovery. However, they informed Aaliyah that they couldn't start treatment immediately because she was pregnant again—just one month along. The news brought a flood of emotions. Aaliyah cried, not knowing how to process the idea of another child while still recovering from the trauma of her first marriage.

But her family stood by her, offering comfort and reassurance. They promised that she would never return to that house, that she would never again be subjected to the horrors she had endured. Her father, Yusuf, was determined to see justice served. He filed charges against Hassan for physical and mental abuse, ensuring that the law would hold him accountable for what he had done.

SCENE 6: THE COURTROOM Showdown

The day of the court trial arrived, and Aaliyah faced Hassan for the first time since she had left his house. Hassan looked thinner, his once-proud demeanour diminished, but his eyes still burned with anger. Salma stood outside the courtroom, hurling accusations and curses at Aaliyah, blaming her for destroying her son's life.

"You'll pay for this, Aaliyah!" Salma shouted. "You won't get away with it!"

But the police quickly intervened, warning Salma to stay quiet or face arrest herself.

In the courtroom, Aaliyah spoke her truth. She described the abuse she had endured, the lies Salma had spread, and the violence Hassan had inflicted upon her. Her words were powerful, and by the end of the trial, the judge ruled in Aaliyah's favour.

Hassan was sentenced to one year in prison for the abuse he had inflicted upon Aaliyah. He was also prohibited from contacting or seeing his sons until they turned five years old, a harsh but necessary consequence for the harm he had caused.

Aaliyah walked out of the courtroom that day with her head held high, knowing that justice had been served. The weight of her past was finally beginning to lift, and she could start to build a new life for herself and her children.

SCENE 7: REBUILDING Life

The next few years were challenging, but they were also filled with healing and growth. Aaliyah gave birth to her second son and found joy in raising her children in the safety and warmth of her family's home. She took on a new role as an Alima at a nearby madrasa, teaching young girls about faith, resilience, and the power of self-worth.

But even as Aaliyah rebuilt her life, the shadows of her past lingered. The nightmares would return from time to time, and she struggled with trust issues. She often locked herself in her room, especially after dark, afraid that Hassan or Salma might somehow find her again

It took years of therapy, prayer, and the support of her family for Aaliyah to fully reclaim her sense of self. Slowly but surely, she began to emerge from the shadows of her trauma, finding peace in her faith and in the love of her children.

SCENE 8: THE RETURN of Hassan

Six months after being released from prison, Hassan was a free man once more. He had hired the best lawyers, pleaded guilty, and served his time. But the experience had changed him in ways that he didn't fully understand.

Hassan returned to a home that no longer felt like his own. Salma, determined to seek revenge on Aaliyah, had arranged for him to remarry. His new wife was from a foreign country, a distant relative whom Salma had chosen specifically for her obedience and lack of ties to Aaliyah's family.

But what Hassan didn't know was that he had another son—Aaliyah had given birth after he had gone to prison, and Salma had kept the truth from him. Salma's hatred for Aaliyah had consumed her, and she used this secret to manipulate Hassan into moving on with his new life.

For Aaliyah, the knowledge that Hassan was free again brought back old fears. But this time, she was stronger, more resilient, and determined to protect herself and her children at all costs.

Chapter 7

Scene 1: The Passage of Time

Two years had passed since Aaliyah's life took a dramatic turn. Her divorce from Hassan was a painful chapter that had come to an end, but the scars—both physical and emotional—still lingered. However, with the unwavering support of her family and her deep faith in Allah, she had slowly begun to heal.

Aaliyah had found purpose in her new role as an Islamic teacher at a local madrasa. Teaching had become her sanctuary, a place where she could share her knowledge of Islam and help guide young minds to faith and resilience. Her students looked up to her, not just because she was knowledgeable, but because she embodied strength and grace even in the face of adversity.

Her eldest son, Adnan, had recently started preschool, coincidentally in the same school where Aaliyah was teaching. It was a joy to see him grow, to watch him laugh and learn, and to know that despite everything they had been through, he was happy and thriving. Aaliyah's second son, Ameen, was just a toddler, but he had a lively spirit that filled their home with joy.

Aaliyah's younger brother, Mohammad, had gone abroad for higher studies, but now he was home for the summer break. His return brought a sense of comfort and familiarity to the household, a reminder that despite the hardships of the past, life was moving forward.

One evening, after dinner, Mohammad approached Aaliyah with a smile on his face.

"Aapi," he said, using the affectionate Urdu term for elder sister, "I want you to meet someone. He's become one of my best friends while I was studying abroad. His name is Zayd, and his family recently moved to our community."

Aaliyah looked at her brother curiously. She had grown used to Mohammad's stories about his friends from university, but this was the first time he had brought one of them home to meet the family.

"Sure, bring him over," Aaliyah said, trying to sound casual, though a hint of anxiety crept into her voice. "It will be nice to meet someone new."

Deep down, Aaliyah still struggled with trusting men after everything she had been through. The wounds from her past marriage had left her cautious and guarded, especially when it came to matters of the heart. But she trusted her brother, and she knew he wouldn't bring someone into their lives unless he was certain they were a good person.

SCENE 2: ZAYD'S INTRODUCTION

RESILIENCE IN THE SHADOWS

The next evening, Mohammad arrived home with Zayd in tow. From the moment Zayd entered the house, Aaliyah noticed something different about him. He had a calm, warm presence that immediately put everyone at ease. He greeted Aaliyah with respect, lowering his gaze politely and speaking in a soft, kind tone.

"As-salamu alaykum," Zayd said with a gentle smile. "It's an honour to meet you, Aaliyah. Mohammad has spoken highly of you and your family."

"Wa alaykum as-salaam," Aaliyah replied, offering a small smile in return. "It's nice to meet you as well."

Zayd was a tall, well-built man with dark hair and kind eyes that reflected his deep faith. He was articulate and well-mannered, and Aaliyah could see why her brother had become friends with him. As the evening went on, Zayd's humour and humility shone through, drawing laughter from both Mohammad and Aaliyah's father, Yusuf.

Though Aaliyah remained quiet for most of the evening, she found herself observing Zayd closely. There was something about his demeanour that intrigued her—something gentle and sincere that she hadn't expected to find in a man again. Zayd wasn't trying to impress anyone; he was simply being himself, and that authenticity was what made him stand out.

But despite her curiosity, Aaliyah kept her guard up. She had been through too much to let her heart become vulnerable so easily. Trust wasn't something she could give freely, not anymore.

Scene 3: Gentle Interactions at the Mosque

Over the following weeks, Zayd's presence became more familiar in the community. His family had settled in nicely, and he quickly became a regular at the local mosque, where he often led prayers and participated in community events. Zayd was devout, but he wasn't rigid or judgmental. His approach to Islam was one of love, compassion, and kindness, which resonated with everyone around him.

It wasn't long before Zayd crossed paths with Aaliyah's sons, Adnan and Ameen, during one of the Friday prayers. Adnan, with his wide eyes and curious nature, had wandered toward the front of the mosque, fascinated by Zayd's calm recitation of the Quran.

After the prayer, Zayd noticed Adnan lingering nearby, watching him with awe. With a smile, Zayd crouched down to Adnan's level.

"As-salamu alaykum, young man, "Zayd said gently. "What brings you here today?"

"Wa alaykum as-salaam," Adnan replied shyly. *"You read the Quran like my Mama. She teaches it at my school."

Zayd chuckled softly, his eyes lighting up at the boy's innocence.

"Your Mama must be a great teacher, then," Zayd said warmly. "What's your name?"

"Adnan," the boy replied proudly. "And that's my little brother, Ameen."

Zayd smiled at Ameen, who was toddling around nearby, and then looked up to see Aaliyah approaching, her face softening as she saw Zayd interacting with her children.

"Ah, so you must be Adnan's mother, "Zayd said as he stood up, offering Aaliyah a warm smile. "Your sons are wonderful, Masha 'Allah."

Aaliyah felt her heart flutter slightly at his words. She wasn't used to receiving compliments about her parenting from men, especially not in such a kind and genuine manner. But she quickly pushed the feeling aside, reminding herself to remain cautious.

"Thank you," Aaliyah said quietly. "They're my world."

Zayd nodded, understanding the depth of her words. He could sense the strength within her, the resilience she had developed over the years. But he also saw the walls she had built around herself—the protective barriers that kept her heart guarded.

Scene 4: Building a Connection

As the weeks turned into months, Aaliyah and Zayd's paths crossed more frequently. Whether it was at the mosque, during community events, or when Zayd would stop by to visit Mohammad, their interactions became more frequent and natural. Zayd never pushed or intruded into Aaliyah's space, but his presence was always respectful and considerate.

He had developed a soft spot for Adnan and Ameen, often playing with them during prayer times or helping Adnan with small tasks at the mosque. Aaliyah watched from a distance, still cautious, but unable to deny that Zayd had a special way with her children. He was patient, kind, and playful in a way that reminded her of what fatherhood should look like.

One day, as Aaliyah was walking home from the mosque with her sons, she noticed Zayd walking in the same direction. They exchanged pleasantries, and soon enough, they were walking together, with Adnan and Ameen running ahead, laughing and playing.

"Your boys are so full of life," Zayd commented with a smile. "It's beautiful to see."

Aaliyah nodded, glancing at her sons with a look of deep love in her eyes.

"They're my strength," she said softly. "I wouldn't have made it through the past few years without them."

Zayd looked at her with understanding in his eyes, sensing the depth of her pain and the strength it had taken for her to rebuild her life.

"You've been through a lot," Zayd said gently, his tone free of judgment. "But I can see that you're strong. You've built a beautiful life for yourself and your children, and that's something to be proud of."

Aaliyah felt a lump form in her throat at his words. She wasn't used to being seen in that way, to having her struggles acknowledged with such kindness. Most people either pitied her or saw her as a broken woman, but Zayd didn't seem to see her that way at all. He saw her as strong, as resilient, as someone who had weathered a storm and come out stronger on the other side.

For the first time in a long while, Aaliyah felt something stir within her heart—a small flicker of warmth that she had thought had long since died out. But even as she felt it, she reminded herself to be cautious. She had been hurt before, and she couldn't afford to let herself fall into that trap again.

"Thank you," she said quietly, offering him a small smile. "That means a lot."

Zayd nodded, understanding her hesitation without needing her to explain it. He respected her boundaries and didn't push for more. He simply walked beside her, content to be a source of support if and when she needed it.

SCENE 5: A GROWING Bond

Over the next few months, Aaliyah's relationship with Zayd continued to develop, though it was slow and steady. Zayd never pressured her for anything more than friendship, and for that, Aaliyah was grateful. He was always kind, always respectful, and always there when she needed help or support.

He became a regular presence in her children's lives, and both Adnan and Ameen grew to adore him. Zayd's light-hearted nature and playful spirit brought joy to their little family, and Aaliyah found herself smiling more often than she had in years.

But despite the growing bond between them, Aaliyah's fears still lingered. She couldn't forget the pain of her past, and the thought of trusting another man with her heart filled her with anxiety. She knew Zayd was different from Hassan—his kindness and compassion were genuine—but the walls she had built around her heart were thick and high.

One evening, after a family dinner at their house, Mohammad sat down with Aaliyah for a private conversation. He had noticed the way Zayd looked at her—the quiet admiration in his eyes—and he wanted to make sure his sister knew that it was okay to open her heart again.

"Aapi," Mohammad said softly, "I know you've been hurt in the past, and I know that it's hard to trust again. But Zayd... he's different. He's a good man. He cares about you and the boys. And I think... I think you deserve to feel loved again."

Aaliyah looked at her brother, her heart heavy with conflicting emotions. She wanted to believe that she could find love again, that she could trust Zayd and build something new with him. But the fear of being hurt again was overwhelming.

"I don't know if I can," Aaliyah admitted, her voice shaking slightly. "What if I let myself care for him, and I end up getting hurt again? I don't think I could survive that."

Mohammad reached out and took her hand, his grip gentle but firm.

"You're stronger than you think, Aapi," he said quietly. "And you don't have to do this alone. You have us—your family—by your side. And from what I've seen, Zayd would never hurt you. He's patient, and he understands what you've been through. Give yourself time. But don't be afraid to let yourself be happy again."

Aaliyah listened to her brother's words, letting them sink in. She knew he was right—she couldn't live in fear forever. Zayd had never given her a reason to doubt him, and perhaps, just maybe, there was a chance that she could find happiness again.

Scene 6: The First Step Toward Love

It took time, but slowly, Aaliyah allowed herself to open up to Zayd. It wasn't easy—each step forward was met with hesitation and uncertainty—but Zayd's patience and understanding made all the difference.

One day, as they sat together at the park, watching Adnan and Ameen play, Aaliyah finally found the courage to speak her heart.

"Zayd," she began, her voice soft but steady, "I don't know what the future holds, and I'm still learning to trust again. But I want you to know that... I appreciate you. Your kindness, your patience... it's helped me more than you know."

Zayd turned to her, his eyes filled with warmth and understanding.

"I'm not asking for anything more than what you're ready to give," Zayd said gently. "All I want is for you to know that I'm here. I care about you, Aaliyah. And I'll wait for as long as it takes."

Aaliyah felt a lump form in her throat, her heart swelling with gratitude. She wasn't ready to say the words just yet, but she knew that Zayd's presence in her life had already begun to heal the wounds of the past. And for the first time in a long time, she felt a glimmer of hope—a hope that maybe, just maybe, she could feel loved again.

As they sat together, watching the sun set over the horizon, Aaliyah allowed herself to relax. She wasn't fully healed yet, but she was on the path to healing. And with Zayd by her side, she knew that she didn't have to walk that path alone.

Chapter 8

The Blossoming of Love

Scene 1: Small Steps Toward Something New

The months following Zayd's arrival into Aaliyah's life were transformative, though the changes were subtle at first. Aaliyah was still cautious, still carrying the weight of her past, but Zayd's constant presence in her life—steady and unassuming—began to wear down the walls she had built around her heart.

Aaliyah continued to teach at the madrasa, focusing on her work and her children. Life had found a sense of normalcy again. Her sons, Adnan and Ameen, were the center of her world. Adnan had grown comfortable in preschool, and Ameen was starting to babble, trying out new words every day. Their laughter filled their home, providing a much-needed balm to Aaliyah's wounded spirit.

But slowly, quietly, Zayd's presence became more than just a comforting backdrop. His kind gestures, his respect for her space, and his ease with her children began to shift something deep inside her. What started as guarded friendship and cautious interaction was transforming into something warmer, something tender.

The first real moment of connection came on a quiet afternoon. Zayd had come to visit Mohammad, and they had spent some time talking in the garden. When Mohammad left to run an errand, Zayd lingered, offering to help Aaliyah with the boys. Aaliyah hesitated at first, but eventually agreed.

As they sat on the porch, watching the boys chase after a ball, Zayd spoke gently, not about anything pressing, but about everyday matters—work, the mosque, his family. His voice was calming, and for the first time in a long while, Aaliyah felt safe in the presence of a man. There was no tension, no expectation—just a natural conversation, two people simply enjoying each other's company.

At one point, Ameen toddled over to Zayd and climbed onto his lap, settling in comfortably as if he had known him forever. Zayd laughed, his eyes crinkling at the corners as he held Ameen with the same tenderness he showed toward everything in life.

"You've got quite the personality, young man," Zayd said, ruffling Ameen's hair. "Just like your mother."

Aaliyah's heart skipped a beat at his words, a blush creeping into her cheeks. She glanced at him, catching the warmth in his gaze, but quickly looked away, still uncertain of what she was feeling. It had been so long since she had felt anything for anyone, and the thought of opening her heart again terrified her.

But in that moment, surrounded by the laughter of her children and the gentle presence of Zayd, Aaliyah allowed herself to entertain the idea that maybe—just maybe—there could be something more.

SCENE 2: A DELICATE Dance

Over the next few weeks, Aaliyah and Zayd's interactions became more frequent and more comfortable. Zayd continued to visit the house, often helping Aaliyah with the boys or simply spending time with her family. Mohammad, ever the supportive brother, encouraged the growing bond between them, though he never pushed or prodded. He understood that Aaliyah needed to move at her own pace.

Zayd was always respectful, never crossing any boundaries that Aaliyah wasn't ready to breach. He never pressured her to talk about her past, though she could tell he was aware of the emotional scars she carried. Instead, he gave her the space to come to him when she was ready, and Aaliyah found herself slowly beginning to trust him more with each passing day.

One evening, after dinner, Aaliyah and Zayd sat together on the porch while the boys played in the yard. The sun was setting, casting a warm glow over the neighbourhood, and the air was filled with the soft hum of crickets.

"You know," Zayd began, his voice thoughtful, "I've seen a lot of strong people in my life, but I've never met anyone quite as strong as you, Aaliyah."

Aaliyah turned to him, surprised by the statement. She wasn't used to being praised for her strength—at least not in a way that felt so sincere.

"I don't know if I'd call myself strong," she said quietly. "I've just... done what I had to do."

Zayd shook his head gently, his eyes soft as he looked at her.

"Surviving is strength," he said. "Raising two boys on your own after everything you've been through—that takes strength. And I see it every time I look at you."

Aaliyah felt her throat tighten with emotion. She had spent so long doubting herself, questioning her worth after everything that had happened with Hassan. She had convinced herself that maybe she wasn't strong enough, that maybe she wasn't deserving of love or kindness. But Zayd's words cut through all of that doubt, reminding her that she was more than just the sum of her past.

"Thank you," Aaliyah whispered, her voice trembling slightly.

Zayd smiled, his expression warm and reassuring.

"You don't have to thank me," he said softly. "I'm just telling the truth."

For the first time in years, Aaliyah felt a sense of peace settle over her. It wasn't just Zayd's words that brought her comfort—it was the way he looked at her, the way he treated her. He saw her as more than just a broken woman or a victim. He saw her as a person with strength, resilience, and value.

And for the first time since her divorce, Aaliyah began to feel a glimmer of something she hadn't felt in a long time: the possibility of love.

SCENE 3: MOMENTS OF Vulnerability

As the weeks continued to pass, Aaliyah found herself opening up more to Zayd. Their conversations deepened, moving beyond casual topics and touching on more personal subjects. Aaliyah shared stories from her childhood, memories of her late mother, and even glimpses of the pain she had endured during her marriage to Hassan.

One evening, after the boys had gone to bed, Aaliyah and Zayd sat together in the living room, the house quiet except for the ticking of the clock on the wall. Aaliyah felt a wave of vulnerability wash over her as she thought about her past, and before she could stop herself, the words came tumbling out.

"I'm scared, Zayd," she admitted, her voice barely above a whisper. "I'm scared of trusting again. I'm scared of opening my heart to someone and being hurt like I was before."

Zayd listened quietly, his gaze never leaving her face. He didn't rush to offer reassurances or platitudes—instead, he gave her the space to speak her truth.

"I know I've been through a lot, Aaliyah continued, her hands twisting nervously in her lap. "And I know that not every man is like Hassan. But... the fear is still there. It's hard to shake."

Zayd reached out and gently took her hand in his, his touch warm and grounding.

"I understand," he said softly. "And I don't want you to feel like you have to rush into anything. Healing takes time, and trust takes time. I'm not here to pressure you into anything, Aaliyah. I'm here because I care about you, and I want to be a part of your life—however that looks."

AALIYAH FELT TEARS prick at the corners of her eyes. She had never expected to find someone like Zayd—someone who was patient, kind, and understanding. Someone who didn't try to fix her but simply stood by her side as she navigated her own healing.

"Thank you," she whispered, her voice thick with emotion. "I've never met anyone like you before."

Zayd smiled, his hand still holding hers.

"And I've never met anyone like you, Aaliyah," he said gently. *"You've been through so much, but you're still standing. That's something to be proud of."

For the first time in a long while, Aaliyah allowed herself to lean into the vulnerability, to let herself be seen and cared for. It wasn't easy—there were still moments of doubt and fear—but Zayd's presence made her feel safe. And in that safety, she found the courage to take small steps toward opening her heart again.

Scene 4: Blossoming Love

As the months continued to pass, Aaliyah's relationship with Zayd deepened. What had started as a tentative friendship blossomed into something more, something beautiful. The love between them grew slowly, like a flower opening its petals to the sun. It wasn't rushed or forced—it was natural, gentle, and filled with mutual respect.

Zayd had become an integral part of Aaliyah's life and her sons' lives as well. Adnan and Ameen adored him, often running to him with laughter and excitement whenever he visited. Zayd's kindness and playfulness brought a new light into their home, and Aaliyah couldn't help but feel grateful for the joy he brought into their lives.

One evening, as they sat together in the garden, watching the boys play, Zayd turned to Aaliyah with a soft expression on his face.

"I want you to know something, Aaliyah," he said quietly. "I've fallen in love with you—not just for your strength, but for who you are. I love the way you care for your sons, the way you carry yourself with grace despite everything you've been through. I love your kindness, your wisdom, your faith. You

are someone I admire deeply, and I would be honoured to stand by your side—if that's something you're ready for."

Aaliyah felt her heart swell with emotion at his words. Tears welled up in her eyes, but this time, they were tears of gratitude, not fear. She had never expected to find love again, especially not after the pain she had endured. But here Zayd was—kind, gentle, and patient—offering her his heart without expecting anything in return.

"I think..." Aaliyah began, her voice trembling slightly, "I think I'm ready to take that step. I'm still healing, but I want to try. I want to open my heart to love again, and I want you to be a part of that."

Zayd smiled, his eyes filled with warmth and affection.

"I'll be with you every step of the way," he said softly. "We'll take it one day at a time, and we'll do it together."

In that moment, Aaliyah felt something shift within her—a sense of peace, of hope. The love that had been slowly blossoming between them had finally taken root, and Aaliyah knew that whatever the future held, she didn't have to face it alone.

Zayd was by her side, and for the first time in years, Aaliyah allowed herself to believe that she was worthy of love, that she could find happiness again. It wouldn't be easy—there would still be challenges to face—but with Zayd's support and the love they had built together, Aaliyah knew that they could weather any storm.

Chapter 9

New Beginnings

Scene 1: A Leap of Faith

After months of healing, growing, and slowly rebuilding her heart, Aaliyah finally found herself ready to take a leap of faith. The past two years had been filled with challenges and moments of doubt, but she had emerged stronger and more certain of her own resilience. Now, with Zayd by her side, the promise of a new beginning was within reach.

Zayd had been patient throughout their journey together. He had never pushed her, never rushed her into anything she wasn't ready for. Instead, he had been a steady presence in her life, showing her kindness and respect at every turn. His love had grown quietly but surely, and as they spent more time together, Aaliyah realized that Zayd was not just someone who loved her—he was someone she could trust with her future.

One evening, while sitting in the garden under a sky filled with stars, Zayd gently broached the subject that had been on both of their minds for some time.

"Aaliyah," he began, his voice soft but steady, *"I've been thinking... about us, about the future. I love you, and I want to spend my life with you and your boys. But I also understand that this decision isn't just about me. It's about you, your children, and what's best for all of you."

Aaliyah looked at him, her heart swelling with emotion. She had known this moment would come eventually, but hearing the words still filled her with a mix of emotions—joy, fear, and excitement all rolled into one.

"I've thought about it too," Aaliyah replied quietly. "And I think... I think I'm ready. I want to take this step with you, Zayd. I want to start a new chapter of my life, with you by my side."

Zayd's face lit up with a smile, his eyes filled with warmth and love. He reached out and took her hand, holding it gently in his.

"We'll do it together, Aaliyah," he said. "One step at a time, with Allah's guidance."

In that moment, Aaliyah felt a sense of peace settle over her. She had been through so much, but she had finally found someone who saw her for who she truly was—someone who valued her, respected her, and loved her unconditionally. And for the first time in years, she felt ready to embrace the future with open arms.

SCENE 2: FAMILY BLESSINGS

The decision to marry Zayd was not one that Aaliyah took lightly. After everything she had been through with Hassan, she knew that trust and love had to be built carefully, brick by brick. But with Zayd, those foundations had already been laid, and now it was time to take the next step.

Before making any formal decisions, Aaliyah wanted to talk to her family. Her father, Yusuf, had always been her pillar of strength, and she valued his opinion deeply. She also wanted to speak with her younger siblings, Mohammad and Safiya, who had supported her through every stage of her recovery.

One evening, after dinner, Aaliyah gathered her family in the living room. She sat with her father, brother, and sister, feeling a mix of nervousness and excitement.

"I have something to tell you," Aaliyah began, glancing around the room at the faces of the people she loved most. "Zayd and I have been talking, and... we've decided that we want to get married."

Yusuf's face broke into a wide smile, his eyes filled with pride.

"Alhamdulillah," he said, his voice filled with emotion. "I've seen how happy Zayd makes you, Aaliyah. He's a good man, and I couldn't be more pleased with this decision. You deserve to be happy, my daughter, and I know that Zayd will take care of you and your sons with love and respect."

Mohammad, always the teasing younger brother, grinned and gave Aaliyah a playful nudge.

"Finally, Aapi!" he said with a chuckle. "I've been waiting for this moment! Zayd is one of the best men I know, and I couldn't be happier for you both."

Safiya, who had always looked up to Aaliyah, threw her arms around her sister, her eyes filled with tears of happiness.

"You deserve this, Aapi,"* she whispered. "You deserve all the happiness in the world."

Aaliyah's heart swelled with love and gratitude for her family. Their support meant everything to her, and knowing that they were behind her decision gave her the strength and confidence she needed to move forward.

Scene 3: A Simple Wedding

When it came time to plan the wedding, Aaliyah and Zayd both agreed on one thing: they wanted it to be simple and meaningful. After everything Aaliyah had been through, she wasn't interested in extravagant celebrations or grand displays. Instead, she wanted a quiet, intimate ceremony surrounded by the people who mattered most.

The wedding took place at the local mosque, with the imam presiding over the nikah ceremony. Aaliyah wore a simple yet elegant white hijab and dress, her heart filled with both nervous anticipation and a deep sense of peace. Her sons, Adnan and Ameen, stood by her side, excited and curious about what was happening. Zayd, dressed in traditional white, stood across from her, his eyes filled with warmth and love.

The ceremony was brief but beautiful. As the imam recited the Quranic verses that bound them together as husband and wife, Aaliyah felt a wave of calm wash over her. This was the start of something new—a fresh chapter, a new beginning, and a chance at happiness that she hadn't thought possible just a few years ago.

When the ceremony was over, Zayd gently took Aaliyah's hand, and together, they walked out of the mosque as husband and wife. The sun was setting in the sky, casting a warm golden light over the world, and Aaliyah couldn't help but smile at the symbolism. The sun was setting on her past, but it was also rising on a new future filled with hope, love, and the promise of happiness.

SCENE 4: ADJUSTING to a New Life

The days that followed the wedding were filled with adjustment, but in the best possible way. Zayd moved into Aaliyah's home, and together, they began to build a life that was rooted in love, respect, and faith. For Aaliyah, this new life felt like a breath of fresh air—a stark contrast to the suffocating and abusive environment she had once endured.

Zayd quickly became a beloved figure in Adnan and Ameen's lives. He treated them as if they were his own sons, taking them to the park, helping them with their studies, and teaching them about Islam in a gentle, loving way. Aaliyah watched as her boys blossomed under Zayd's care, and her heart swelled with gratitude.

But as with any new beginning, there were challenges. Aaliyah still had moments of fear and anxiety, remnants of the trauma she had endured during her first marriage. There were nights when she woke up in a panic, haunted by nightmares of Hassan's abuse. But Zayd was always there, patient and understanding, holding her through the difficult moments and reminding her that she was safe now.

"We'll get through this together," Zayd would say, his voice steady and reassuring. "You're not alone anymore, Aaliyah. I'm here, and I always will be."

With Zayd's support, Aaliyah slowly began to heal on a deeper level. She had already done so much work to rebuild her life after her divorce, but now, with Zayd by her side, she felt a sense of completeness that she hadn't known was possible.

SCENE 5: BLOSSOMING Love

RESILIENCE IN THE SHADOWS

As the months passed, Aaliyah and Zayd's love deepened. What had started as a friendship rooted in mutual respect and admiration had blossomed into a full-fledged love story. Zayd's gentle nature, his unwavering faith, and his devotion to Aaliyah and her sons made her fall in love with him more each day.

One afternoon, as they sat together in the garden, Aaliyah turned to Zayd with a smile.

"Do you ever think about how far we've come?" she asked, her voice filled with wonder. "I never imagined that I could find love again after everything that happened with Hassan. But now, with you... I feel like I've been given a second chance at happiness."

Zayd smiled, taking her hand in his.

"I think about it all the time," he said softly. "I think about how blessed I am to have you in my life. You've taught me so much about strength, resilience, and faith. And I'm grateful every day that Allah brought us together."

Aaliyah's heart swelled with emotion. She had once thought that love was something that would always elude her, that her past had left her too broken to ever experience true happiness. But now, sitting beside Zayd, surrounded by the laughter of her children, she realized that love was not just something she deserved—it was something she had been blessed with.

"I love you, Zayd," Aaliyah whispered, her voice filled with sincerity.

Zayd's eyes softened as he looked at her, his heart overflowing with love.

"And I love you, Aaliyah," he said, pulling her closer. "Always."

In that moment, Aaliyah knew that this was what

true love felt like—peaceful, steady, and full of grace. It wasn't about grand gestures or sweeping declarations. It was about the quiet moments of connection, the deep trust they had built, and the unwavering support they gave each other. It was about building a life together, rooted in faith and love, and finding joy in the simple, everyday moments.

SCENE 6: THE PROMISE of a New Future

As time went on, Aaliyah and Zayd's life continued to flourish. They faced challenges together, but they also celebrated the joys of life—Adnan's first day of primary school, Ameen learning new words, and the simple pleasure of family dinners filled with laughter and love.

Aaliyah's life had come full circle. She had once been trapped in a cycle of abuse, fear, and pain, but now, she was free. She had built a life that was filled with love, faith, and the promise of a bright future. And though the scars of her past would always be a part of her, they no longer defined her. She was stronger than her pain, more resilient than her trauma, and more deserving of love than she had ever believed.

With Zayd by her side, Aaliyah felt ready to embrace whatever the future held. Together, they would continue to build a life rooted in love, respect, and faith—a life that honoured the strength and resilience that had brought them together in the first place.

And as Aaliyah looked toward that future, she did so with hope, gratitude, and a heart full of love.

Chapter 10

A New Legacy

Scene 1: Confronting the Past

Two years had passed since Aaliyah and Zayd began their new life together. Their home had become a sanctuary of love, laughter, and peace—a stark contrast to the life Aaliyah had once known. The boys had flourished under Zayd's care, and Aaliyah had blossomed into a strong, confident woman who was no longer defined by her past. Together, they were building a legacy of faith, compassion, and resilience.

Yet, despite the peace she had found, there was still one piece of her past that remained unresolved—Hassan and his mother, Salma. For years, they had haunted her thoughts like distant shadows, always lurking in the background but never quite disappearing. Aaliyah had moved on with her life, but she knew that in order to fully heal, she would eventually have to confront the ghosts of her past.

The opportunity came unexpectedly one afternoon.

Aaliyah was sitting in the garden with Zayd and the boys when the doorbell rang. Zayd excused himself to answer it, expecting a friend or neighbour, but when he opened the door, he was met with the sight of two familiar faces: Hassan and Salma.

Zayd's expression hardened immediately, protective instincts kicking in as he stood between Aaliyah's past and her present. Hassan looked different—thinner, worn down by life's hardships—and Salma seemed frail, her once authoritative presence diminished by the weight of time and regret. They both stood awkwardly at the door, unsure of how to begin.

"As-salamu alaykum," Hassan said, his voice hesitant and unsure.

Zayd didn't return the greeting immediately. Instead, he stood in silence, his protective nature keeping him on guard. He didn't trust Hassan—he didn't believe that someone capable of causing such pain could ever truly change.

Aaliyah, however, had overheard the conversation from the garden. She stepped forward, her heart pounding in her chest as she came face-to-face with the people who had once caused her so much harm. She hadn't seen Hassan or Salma in years, and the sight of them now—so changed, so humbled—stirred a complicated mix of emotions within her.

"What do you want?" Aaliyah asked, her voice steady but firm. She wasn't the same woman she had been all those years ago. She wasn't afraid anymore.

Hassan looked down at the ground, shame washing over his features.

"We... we came to ask for forgiveness," he said quietly. "I know that what I did was unforgivable, but... I've spent the last few years reflecting on my mistakes. My second marriage ended in divorce, and... I realized that I've lost everything. It was all my fault. I hurt you in ways that I can never take back, but... I want to make amends."

Salma, too, spoke up, her voice weaker than Aaliyah remembered.

"I was wrong, Aaliyah," she said, her tone filled with regret. "I was blinded by my pride and my desire to control everything. I took my anger and fear out on you, and I destroyed my own family in the process. I've lost my sons, and I've lost my grandchildren. Please... if there is any room in your heart for forgiveness, I beg of you to forgive us."

Aaliyah stood there, her heart racing as she listened to their words. The pain of her past still lingered, but it no longer controlled her. She had moved on, built a new life for herself and her children, and found love in ways she never thought possible. Yet, the idea of forgiveness was something she had struggled with for a long time.

Could she forgive them? Could she release the burden of the anger she had carried for so many years?

Zayd, sensing Aaliyah's inner turmoil, gently placed a hand on her shoulder.

"This is your decision, Aaliyah," he said softly. *"Whatever you choose, I will support you."

Aaliyah closed her eyes for a moment, taking a deep breath. Forgiveness wasn't just about absolving the people who had hurt her—it was about freeing herself from the chains of her past. She had already built a new life, but now she had the chance to let go of the bitterness that had once consumed her.

When she opened her eyes, she looked at Hassan and Salma with a sense of calm that surprised even her.

"I forgive you," Aaliyah said quietly. "Not because you deserve it, but because I deserve peace. I've spent too long holding on to anger, and it's time for me to let go. May Allah forgive us all for our mistakes and guide us to better lives."

Hassan and Salma looked at Aaliyah with tears in their eyes, overwhelmed by her mercy. They had come expecting rejection, but instead, they were met with compassion and grace. They thanked her profusely, but Aaliyah simply nodded, knowing that her journey with them had finally come to an end.

SCENE 2: THE GIFT OF a New Life

As Aaliyah turned back toward the garden, she felt a sense of relief wash over her. The confrontation with Hassan and Salma had been a test of her strength, but it had also been an opportunity for closure. She had forgiven them, not for their sake, but for her own. And now, she could move forward with her life, free of the shadows that had once held her back.

But little did Aaliyah know, her life was about to take yet another beautiful turn.

A few weeks after Hassan and Salma's visit, Aaliyah began to feel unusual symptoms—nausea, fatigue, and a sudden craving for certain foods. At first, she dismissed it as stress or exhaustion, but when the symptoms persisted, Zayd gently suggested that she visit the doctor for a check-up.

To Aaliyah's surprise, the doctor delivered news that she hadn't expected: she was pregnant.

A wave of emotions flooded Aaliyah's heart as she processed the news. She hadn't thought about having more children—after everything she had been through, she had been content with her two boys and the new life she had built. But now, with this new life growing inside her, Aaliyah felt a sense of awe and wonder. It was as if Allah had given her yet another chance to create something beautiful out of the ashes of her past.

When Aaliyah told Zayd the news, his face lit up with joy.

"A baby? "he asked, his voice filled with excitement. "Alhamdulillah! This is such a blessing, Aaliyah. I can't wait to meet our little one."

Aaliyah smiled, feeling a warmth spread through her heart. This new baby was a gift—a symbol of the new life they were building together, a legacy of love, faith, and resilience that would continue to grow and flourish.

SCENE 3: A COMMUNITY Grows

As Aaliyah's pregnancy progressed, the entire community rallied around her. The women from the madrasa where she taught brought her food, checked in on her regularly, and helped with her boys when she needed rest. Zayd, ever the supportive husband, took on more responsibilities at home, making sure that Aaliyah had everything she needed to stay healthy and comfortable.

The love and support that surrounded Aaliyah during her pregnancy was a testament to the life she had built. She had once been isolated, trapped in a marriage that suffocated her spirit, but now she was part of a thriving community that valued her, respected her, and loved her.

Her boys, Adnan and Ameen, were excited about the arrival of their new sibling. They often asked questions about the baby, wondering whether they would have a little brother or sister. Zayd loved to play along, teasing them with imaginative stories about what their new sibling would be like.

"Maybe the baby will be a soccer player," Zayd joked one evening as they sat around the dinner table. "Or maybe a famous scholar who will travel the world spreading knowledge."

Adnan giggled. "Or maybe the baby will be a chef who makes the best desserts in the world!" he said excitedly.

Aaliyah laughed, her heart filled with joy as she watched her family's excitement grow with each passing day.

SCENE 4: A LASTING Legacy

As Aaliyah neared the end of her pregnancy, she began to reflect on the journey she had been on—the pain, the healing, the love, and the growth that had defined the past few years. She had faced so many challenges, but she had also been blessed with so many opportunities to build something new, something lasting.

One afternoon, as she sat with Zayd in the garden, watching the boys play, she turned to him with a thoughtful expression.

"I've been thinking a lot about the future," Aaliyah said softly. "About the legacy we want to leave behind for our children."

Zayd nodded, his eyes filled with love as he looked at her.

"What have you been thinking?" he asked.

Aaliyah took a deep breath, her heart swelling with gratitude for the life they had built together.

"I want our legacy to be one of love, faith, and resilience," she said. "I want our children to know that no matter what challenges they face, they can overcome them with the help of Allah and the support of their family. I want them to grow up knowing that they are loved, valued, and capable of creating something beautiful out of even the darkest moments."

Zayd smiled, taking her hand in his.

"That's exactly the kind of legacy I want to leave behind," he said. "And I know that with you by my side, we can create that legacy together."

SCENE 5: THE ARRIVAL of a New Gift

One crisp autumn morning, after months of anticipation, Aaliyah went into labour. The house was filled with a sense of excitement and nervous energy as Zayd prepared to take her to the hospital. Adnan and Ameen were left in the care of Aaliyah's family, who had come to support them during this special time.

After several hours of labour, Aaliyah gave birth to a healthy baby girl. When the nurse placed the tiny bundle in Aaliyah's arms, tears filled her eyes. She looked down at her daughter, overwhelmed by the miracle of new life.

"She's beautiful," Zayd whispered, standing beside Aaliyah and gazing at their daughter with love in his eyes. "Alhamdulillah. She's a gift from Allah."

Aaliyah smiled through her tears, feeling a deep sense of peace and joy. This baby girl was a symbol of everything she had worked for, everything she had fought to protect. She was the embodiment of the new legacy that Aaliyah and Zayd were building—a legacy of love, faith, and resilience.

They named her Noor, which means "light" in Arabic. And as Aaliyah held Noor in her arms, she knew that this baby would grow up surrounded by the warmth and love of a family that had been built on the foundations of faith and healing.

SCENE 6: THE FUTURE is Bright

As the days turned into weeks and Noor grew stronger, Aaliyah and Zayd found themselves settling into a new rhythm as a family of five. Their home was filled with laughter, love, and the joyful chaos that comes with raising children.

Aaliyah often reflected on how far she had come—from the darkness of her past to the light of her present. She had faced so many challenges, but she had emerged stronger, more resilient, and more determined to create a life filled with love and faith.

Now, as she watched her children grow, Aaliyah knew that the legacy she and Zayd were building would continue for generations to come. It was a legacy rooted in forgiveness, healing, and the belief that no matter what hardships life throws your way, you have the power to rise above them.

And as she held Noor close, Aaliyah whispered a prayer of gratitude, thanking Allah for the blessings that had been bestowed upon her. She knew that the future was bright, and she was ready to embrace it with open arms.

END.....

Inspiration for Those Who Have Lost Faith in Life and Love

THE STORY OF AALIYAH'S journey is one of immense resilience, hope, and the power of faith. It speaks to anyone who has experienced pain, betrayal, or loss and offers a message of renewal, healing, and the possibility of a brighter future. If you find yourself struggling to believe in life or love again, Aaliyah's story serves as a reminder of the strength that resides within all of us.

Here are some key takeaways from her journey that can inspire anyone who has lost faith:

1. Healing Takes Time, and That's Okay.

Aaliyah's story shows that healing is not immediate. She endured unimaginable pain and hardship during her first marriage, and her journey to recovery was slow and challenging. It took years for her to rebuild her sense of self, to trust again, and to feel whole. This reminds us that healing is a gradual process and that it's okay to take time to heal from our wounds. Every small step toward recovery is a victory in itself.

2. Strength Is Found in Vulnerability

Aaliyah's greatest strength came from her ability to be vulnerable. She wasn't afraid to admit her fears, her doubts, and her hesitations. Her openness allowed her to receive the support and love she needed to heal. Being vulnerable doesn't make you weak; it is, in fact, an act of courage. It opens the door to deeper connections and allows others to lift you when you need help the most.

3. Faith Can Be a Guiding Light

Throughout her trials, Aaliyah remained rooted in her faith. Her belief in Allah and in the power of divine guidance gave her strength when she felt weakest. For anyone who feels lost, faith—whether in a higher power, in oneself, or in the potential for goodness in life—can be a beacon that guides you through the darkest of times. Faith reminds us that there is always hope, even when we can't yet see it.

4. Love Can Be Found After Pain

Aaliyah's story demonstrates that even after heartbreak and betrayal, love can be found again. Real love—built on mutual respect, patience, and kindness—can heal even the deepest wounds. Zayd's entrance into Aaliyah's life shows that it's possible to love again, even when you're scared, and that the right person will honour your healing process rather than rush it. Love after pain is possible, and it can be even more profound because of the strength it requires.

5. Forgiveness Is Freedom

Forgiveness is central to Aaliyah's story. She forgave Hassan and Salma, not because they deserved it, but because she deserved peace. Holding on to anger and resentment only binds us to the past. Letting go of that burden, even if it's incredibly hard, can free us to live fully in the present and to embrace the future with open arms. Forgiveness isn't about excusing the wrongs that were done; it's about choosing to no longer let them control your life.

6. A New Beginning Is Always Possible

Aaliyah's journey shows that no matter how dark the past may have been, a new beginning is always possible. Her life with Zayd, her children, and her new daughter, Noor, is a testament to the fact that we can rebuild, reclaim our happiness, and create a life that is full of love and joy, even after the most difficult of times. The past does not define the future, and we always have the power to create a new story for ourselves.

7. You Are Worthy of Love and Happiness

At the heart of Aaliyah's story is a powerful message: you are worthy of love and happiness, no matter what you have been through. Aaliyah had to learn to believe this herself after years of abuse and self-doubt, but once she did, she opened herself up to a life filled with joy, fulfillment, and the kind of love she had always deserved. You, too, are worthy of love—both from others and from yourself.

Conclusion: Hope in Every Chapter in your life

Aaliyah's story is a reminder that life is a series of chapters, and even when one chapter is filled with pain and struggle, the next chapter can be filled with light, love, and growth. If you are struggling with faith in life or love, remember that this is just one chapter in your story. There are new beginnings waiting for you, filled with possibilities you may not yet see.

Keep going, hold on to faith, and know that love—whether it's from a partner, family, friends, or from within yourself—is possible after even the darkest of times. The best chapters of your life may still be ahead.

THANK YOU FOR READING MY BOOK.........

Don't miss out!

Visit the website below and you can sign up to receive emails whenever Nazreen zainab publishes a new book. There's no charge and no obligation.

https://books2read.com/r/B-A-NKTJC-VTFZE

BOOKS 2 READ

Connecting independent readers to independent writers.

Did you love *RESILIENCE IN THE SHADOWS*? Then you should read *Deception in Bloom* by Nazreen zainab!

"Deception in Bloom" is a captivating tale that weaves romance, suspense, and mystery into an unforgettable story of love and betrayal.

Cat Sinclair thought she had met the perfect man in the charming and mysterious Ryan Winters. Their chemistry was undeniable, their connection instant, and their love story seemed destined for greatness. But as their relationship blossoms, shadows begin to creep in. Strange occurrences, hidden secrets, and ghostly visions haunt Cat's once perfect world.

As she delves deeper into Ryan's past, Cat uncovers a web of deception that threatens to unravel everything she thought she knew about him. Torn between her heart and the dark truth, she must decide if love is worth the risk—even if it could destroy her.

Filled with heart-pounding twists, steamy romance, and haunting mysteries, "Deception in Bloom" is a thrilling novel that will keep readers on the edge of their seats. This is a story of passion, lies, and the dangerous allure of love when trust is broken and nothing is as it seems.

Perfect for fans of romantic thrillers with a dark, supernatural twist, "Deception in Bloom" will have you guessing until the very last page.

Also by Nazreen zainab

Deception in Bloom
RESILIENCE IN THE SHADOWS

www.ingramcontent.com/pod-product-compliance
Lightning Source LLC
Chambersburg PA
CBHW051901130726

47987CB00002B/926